THE ANGEL HUNT

DARK WORLD: THE ANGEL TRIALS 2

MICHELLE MADOW

DREAMSCAPE PUBLISHING

"*I* can't believe we left Margo by the side of the freeway in the middle of nowhere, Texas," Sage mourned the loss of her Range Rover—the car she'd named Margo—as we sped down the road.

I had a feeling she wasn't going to get over this anytime soon, as evidenced by the way she was pouting in the driver seat of the truck we'd stolen from the coyote shifters who'd attacked us.

Except... can you really *steal* if the previous owner was dead? Because dead people can't own things.

Correction: The truck we'd *inherited* from the coyote shifters who'd attacked us.

The coyotes certainly hadn't intended to leave the truck to us. But after what they'd put us through, we deserved it. Because after they'd surrounded us and driven us off the empty freeway in the middle of nowhere, they'd launched an attack against Noah, Sage, and me.

Well, they hadn't known I was there since I was hiding in the Range Rover. So the attack had been against Sage and Noah. But still. They'd cornered us and attacked us.

Noah and Sage had *sworn* it would be easy to defeat the coyotes. After all, two oversized, ferocious wolves against a pack of coyotes? The victor should have been a no brainer.

They hadn't counted on one of the coyotes being a dyad—a shifter who can shift into two different animal forms. From what Noah and Sage had told me, dyads were rare, since a shifter only became a dyad when they mated with a shifter of a different species. The mating process joined both their souls together, allowing them to access both forms.

The dyad in the pack that had attacked us could shift into both a coyote *and* a mountain lion.

Wolves could easily beat coyotes.

Mountain lions? Not so much.

Luckily, I'd had a moment of ingenuity in which I'd downed a vial of invisibility potion and distracted the coyotes, giving Noah and Sage the opportunity they'd needed to go in for the kill.

Except judging by the way Noah was brooding at me from the back seat of the truck, he still didn't appreciate my help. If it were up to him, I'd have stayed hidden and out of danger. He wanted me to be a damsel in distress who sat to the side and let others fight battles for her.

I was no damsel. Sitting to the side and not taking action *so* wasn't my style.

But Noah had made it clear that since I was a human, he saw me as useless. I thought helping in that fight would have changed his mind, but apparently not.

Stupid, stubborn wolf shifter.

"We need more AC." I fiddled with the knob, determined to ignore Noah's death stares. You'd think from the way he was glaring at me that I'd tried to kill him— not save him. "This can't be the highest it goes."

Unfortunately, judging by the tiny wisps of air fighting their way out of the vents, it appeared that *was* the highest it went.

"We can always lower the windows," Noah said. "It'll be nice to travel in silence for a change."

"*Burn*." I rolled my eyes, refusing to allow him to get to me. "I'd regret saving your life if I didn't need your help getting to Avalon."

Avalon. The island the vampire psychic Rosella had told me to go to gain the strength I needed to save my mom from Azazel—the greater demon who'd abducted her.

I had no idea what a greater demon wanted with my mom. But I wouldn't rest until she was safe.

To gain entrance to Avalon, Noah needed to present ten demon teeth to its ruler—an angel named Annika. *Why* he needed to do this was beyond me. Noah wasn't a man of many words, so I had no idea why he'd been given this special task. But Rosella had told me that to get to Avalon and have the best chance of saving my mom, I needed to join him on his hunt for demons.

He currently had six demon teeth, which meant he had four to go.

So here I was. In a piece of crap pickup truck rattling down the freeway with two wolf shifters who'd made it clear that this mission would be a lot easier for them if they didn't have me—a human—dragging them down.

At least unlike some shifters, they had control of their human sides. If they didn't, I'd be in danger of becoming a convenient meal on the road.

I supposed I should have been scared of them. But I wasn't. Sage was cool, and while Noah and I were constantly butting heads, he wouldn't hurt me. He'd had enough chances by now that I knew I was safe with him.

"*If* you'd saved my life—which you didn't, by the way

—you wouldn't regret it." Noah smirked. "You like me too much."

"I do not." I bristled and turned away from him, keeping my gaze straight out at the road ahead and refusing to look back at him. Partly because he was irritating me, and partly because it was true.

But mainly because even if I *did* like Noah, it wouldn't matter. Shifters imprinted on other shifters, and eventually chose one of the shifters they'd imprinted on to be their mate. Once they chose a mate, their hearts belonged to each other forever. They'd never mate again, even if their mate died.

Since I was a human and shifters couldn't imprint on humans, I wasn't in the running for Noah's affections. At least not if I wanted to be anything more than a fling. Which I didn't. So yeah—liking him was out of the question.

Especially since I had more important things to focus on—like saving my mom.

"You also wouldn't regret saving my life because you owe me," he added. "Or have you already forgotten that I saved your life—for *real*—from the demon who attacked you in that alley?"

"The coyote I killed to distract the others was real." I turned back around and gripped the seat, anger blazing in my eyes. I still hadn't grappled with the fact that the coyote I'd killed was a shifter—which meant it had a human form—but I'd deal with that another day. "It wasn't a coincidence that you killed that mountain lion immediately afterward. I helped you in that fight, whether you want to admit it or not."

"Maybe I should have let Eli hand you off to Azazel in that alley," he muttered, crossing his arms and turning away from me. "It would have been a lot easier than babysitting a bullheaded human who can't sit back and do what she's told."

"Bullheaded?" I raised an eyebrow. "Personally, I think 'stubborn' is a much better description of me. *You're* the bullheaded one, since you refuse to acknowledge that I helped you."

"And you still think you know best," he said. "Even though you've only known about the supernatural world for what—a few days?"

"Stop it!" Sage snapped. "Both of you. I get it—none of us are happy right now. We had to abandon Margo for a piece of crap truck that has terrible AC, a radio that barely works, and no way to charge our phones. This is *not* the way a Montgomery road trips. But the two of you fighting about the past is distracting us from the elephant in the room here."

As far as I was aware, there were only wolves in the

room—no elephants. But I knew better than to voice that thought out loud.

"What elephant in the room?" I asked instead, more than eager for the change of subject.

"The fact that the coyote attack wasn't random," she said. "They were after me, and seeing as they're all dead now, none of us know why."

*O*f *course*, I thought, remembering the conversation I'd overheard between Sage, Noah, and the coyotes before they'd attacked. The coyotes had specifically said they needed Sage Montgomery to come with them.

They'd known her name, even though she hadn't introduced herself to them.

"Had you ever met those coyotes before?" I asked.

"Never," she said.

"But they knew who you were," I continued. "And they knew how to find you."

"Bravo." Noah slow clapped from his seat in back. "The human's able to string together a few simple facts."

"That's rich coming from you." I turned around,

gripped the back of the chair again, and glared. I refused to take this treatment from him anymore. Not like I ever accepted it to begin with, but there was a line, and he had *way* over-crossed by now.

"Coming from me?" he repeated, raising an eyebrow. "What do you mean by that?"

Coming from someone who doesn't know how to read, I thought. But I pressed my lips together, not saying it out loud. I wouldn't stoop that low. It was too mean, despite the crappy way Noah was treating me.

I didn't know much about his background, but it was clear that his not knowing how to read was because of how he grew up. And judging by the few conversations we'd had so far, he only left his home a few weeks ago, when he started on his demon hunt and met up with Sage.

His not knowing how to read wasn't his fault.

But being born human wasn't my fault, either.

"I just meant that you haven't exactly come up with an answer, either," I said instead. "Unless you know something you're not telling us?"

"Now that you ask, no—I don't know why the coyotes were after Sage," he said. "But I *do* have an idea of how they might have been able to track us."

"How?" Sage asked. "Because with our cloaking

rings, tracking either of us is impossible. And we've both had our rings on since leaving the Montgomery complex."

"Except when you gave yours to Raven before we fought the coyotes," Noah said. "But they'd already tracked us by then, so that's not relevant."

"So how do you think they tracked you?" I was just as eager to hear his theory as Sage.

"I don't think they were tracking Sage or me." His gaze snapped to mine. "I think they were tracking you."

"Me?" I choked, barely able to contain a chuckle. It wasn't funny—it just made no sense. "Why would they be tracking me?"

"To get to Sage." He sat back in his seat, looking mighty proud of himself for his deduction. "Whoever sent them must know we're traveling with a human. All they'd have to do was go to your apartment and get something of yours to be able to track you."

"Hold up," I said, since this was getting more and move convoluted by the second. "Now not only do these people looking for Sage know that I'm traveling with you, but they know where I *live*?"

"It's just a guess," he said. "Do you have a better one?"

"No," I said, since obviously I didn't. The whole supernatural world was brand new to me, which made me as clueless as ever. Noah knew that.

He only asked me that question to get under my skin.

"They could be using a tracking chip," I threw the idea out there, since it was better than sitting there like a mute idiot. "You know—the way *humans* track people."

"Supernaturals don't use technology for stuff like that," he said simply. "Magic is far more reliable. Besides, Azazel knew where you lived. I don't think it's too far out there to think that whoever's looking for Sage figured it out too."

"What would Azazel want with me?" Sage asked. "He doesn't even know who I am. And even if Azazel *were* after me, why would the coyotes work with him? They hate him just as much as we do."

"Relax," Noah said, although given our current predicament, it seemed impossible for *any* of us to relax. "I never said Azazel was after you. Maybe it's Azazel, maybe not. The point here is that since Raven doesn't have a cloaking ring, her being with us is putting us in danger from whoever *is* after you."

"Of course." I rolled my eyes. "It always comes back to another way I'm messing up your mission and putting you in danger."

"Don't take it so personally," Noah said. "Especially since unlike you being human, this problem has an actual solution."

"Oh yeah?" I asked. "What solution is that?"

"It's simple." He smirked, and I cursed my heart for the way it pounded harder when he looked at me like that. "Once we get to New Orleans and go to the witch there, we'll get you a cloaking ring of your own."

FLINT

I paced around my room—the master bedroom in the Montgomery compound—glaring at the phone in my hand.

The first bits of light were starting to peak over the tops of the Hollywood Hills outside my window, but I hadn't gotten a wink of sleep all night. Because the coyotes should have contacted me by now to let me know that they had Sage and were on their way back to LA. There shouldn't have been any problems. The plan had been airtight.

After all, there had been no question which route Sage, Noah, and the human were taking to New Orleans. Straight east on the 10. And that road got pretty deserted all the way out in the middle of nowhere in Southwest Texas. *Especially* at night.

The coyotes—plus that handy dyad mountain lion of theirs—should have been waiting to ambush them the moment they spotted the Range Rover. They were to take Sage, kill her companions, and bring her to me.

I'd offered such a generous monetary reward for the completion of the task that they'd jumped at the job. Coyotes were such a greedy, pathetic, predictable bunch.

I'd tried calling their leader, Wyatt, multiple times to check in and see how it was going. Each time, it rang through to voicemail. He was ignoring me. The question was—why?

I picked up the phone and called Wyatt again.

It rang through to voicemail. Again.

Rage coursed through my veins. I gripped the phone tighter, seconds away from throwing it against the wall.

But that wouldn't help anything. So I took a deep breath and thought about this logically. Wyatt's number wasn't the only one I had from the coyote pack. In case of an emergency, he'd given me the number of their matriarch, Glenda. According to Wyatt, Glenda was so old that she couldn't fight anymore, and she kept herself on top of all the drama of their pack.

I searched for Glenda in my contacts and called her.

She picked up on the first ring. "Hello?" Her voice was low and gravelly—not what I'd expected.

"Is this Glenda of the Southwest Texas coyote pack?" I asked.

"This is she." She left it at that—I wasn't sure if she knew who I was or not.

Best to state my business, and state it quickly.

"This is Flint Montgomery, alpha of the Montgomery wolf pack," I started. No need to specify that the pack was in LA—*every* shifter knew that the Montgomery pack was in LA. "Some of your boys are out doing a job for me."

"I know who you are." She sounded sharper now. More on edge. "If you called to apologize, forget it. And don't call back here ever again."

"Wait!" I yelled into the phone, afraid she was going to hang up.

I glanced at the screen, relieved to see she was still on the line.

"Yeah?" From her tone, I could practically imagine her giving me one hell of a nasty side-eye.

"I should have heard from Wyatt by now, but I seem to be unable to make contact with him," I said, returning to my default way of speaking. Cool, relaxed, and in control. "Do you have any updates on his status?"

"You haven't heard." Her voice was flat. "Of *course* you haven't heard. How could you have?"

"Haven't heard what?" I froze, my lungs tightening with dread.

"Wyatt's dead," she said simply. "All of the shifters who went on the mission with him are dead."

"What?" I asked, shocked.

"You heard me," she said. "I felt their life forces die out about two hours ago. I don't know what type of mission you sent my boys on, but it killed them. *All* of them."

I didn't speak for a few seconds, too stunned to respond. There was certainly no need to ask how she knew they were dead. Pack mates had a spiritual connection to each other. When one member of the pack died, the rest of the pack felt their soul disappear. It was cold when it happened, like falling into icy water and having your lungs robbed of air. The feeling only lasted for a second, but when it happened, it felt like the longest second of your life. And we instinctively knew *which* member of the pack had just lost his or her life. It was impossible to describe how we knew—we just knew it in our bones.

Wyatt and the others were dead.

Sage was still alive.

I was glad my sister was alive, but her being alive meant only one thing—Sage, Noah, and that wretched redheaded human traveling with them had killed the coyotes. All of them. Even the mountain lion dyad.

I knew my sister was a strong fighter, but damn. As angry as I was that Wyatt and his boys had failed, I was impressed by her skills.

Hopefully Azazel would be impressed, too.

"I'm sorry for your loss," I told Glenda, even though I couldn't care less. "I'll respect your wishes and won't call again."

Why *would* I call again, when her pack was a bunch of imbeciles who couldn't manage to take down two wolf shifters and a human, even with a *mountain lion* on their side?

I hung up before she could reply and threw my phone onto my bed, pacing around my room some more while running my fingers through my hair. It was a relief that Sage was alive, but my sister sure wasn't making this easy on me. She was probably nearly to New Orleans by now.

If she were going to any other city, I could send another pack to ambush her. But not New Orleans.

Because New Orleans was home to the rougarou. Fierce fighters, all of them. They were the only wolf pack in the entire country as strong as mine.

Needless to say, the rougarou and the Montgomerys were *not* on good terms. We had a deal—we'd stay out of

New Orleans, and they'd stay out of LA. It was risky enough that Sage was venturing onto their territory. With her cloaking ring, they wouldn't know she was there, but it was still dangerous.

If I called the rougarou alpha and asked to make a deal with her in exchange for the rougarou getting Sage back to LA, she'd laugh in my face. Then she'd likely search down Sage, do what the coyotes couldn't, and mail my sister's head to me in a box.

To keep Sage alive, the rougarou couldn't know that a member of the Montgomery pack was on their territory.

In the meantime, I needed to figure out what to tell Azazel. Last I'd spoken to him, I'd assured him that Sage would be back home in no time. Once she was back, the Montgomery pack would bind ourselves to the greater demon. By binding ourselves to him, we'd be demonstrating our loyalty to the side that would inevitably win this war—the demons. And I'd finally be able to mate with Mara, the perfect, beautiful demon I'd imprinted upon.

After I'd sung Sage's praises to Azazel, he'd agreed to postpone the binding ceremony until her return. Showing him her picture hadn't hurt, either. I wasn't an idiot—I knew men found my sister attractive. And apparently, despite being a greater demon, Azazel was also a typical man.

But he wouldn't wait forever.

Sage was stubborn—she wouldn't abandon Noah on his hunt. So I needed to get her back to LA as quickly as possible.

Then, once she was back, the blood binding ceremony could begin.

RAVEN

*T*he rusted pickup truck we'd stolen from the coyotes hardly belonged on the *road*, yet alone on the rounded drive of the luxurious Ritz-Carlton hotel in New Orleans. Yet here we were, surrounded by a slew of expensive cars and limos, looking as out of place as ever.

We stood out like a mountain lion in a pack of coyotes.

A woman in a fitted dress suit stepped out of the limo in front of us, walking gracefully in red-bottomed heels toward the grand entrance. With her perfectly coiffed hair, she looked like she belonged on a Hollywood movie set in the forties.

I glanced down at my jeans and tried to rub off the splotch of blood that had landed above my knee when

I'd stabbed the coyote's neck. The blood was hard now. A bit of it flaked off, but the stain remained.

Maybe it could pass at the latest fashion statement? After all, purposefully ripped jeans were a thing. Who was to say that splotches of blood wouldn't be the next hot trend?

Fake blood, of course. Not blood from the coyote shifter I'd callously murdered to save my friends from having their heads ripped off by a mountain lion.

It was technically self-defense, but still. I'd never killed anything before. Especially not something human. Well, half human. Sage and Noah had assured me multiple times on the drive here that I shouldn't feel bad about it, but it didn't change the fact that I'd ended a life.

If we hadn't been on this dangerous mission to hunt demons to save my mom, I probably would have broken down about it by now. But we *were* on this mission. And if I wanted to save my mom, I needed to get my act together.

Maybe this was what Rosella had meant when she'd said I would need the experience from the demon hunt if I wanted a chance of surviving the Angel Trials on Avalon.

I still had no idea what the Angel Trials actually *were*, of course. But that was a question for another day.

It was a question I'd ask the Earth Angel herself once we reached Avalon.

In the meantime, I needed to focus on the present—where white-gloved men working the valet stand watched us with wide eyes as we pulled to a stop in front of the hotel. Two of them looked at each other, and the older of them walked around to the driver side of our vehicle.

I expected him to open the door for Sage. Instead, he motioned for her to lower the window.

She reached down for the crank handle—yes, the truck was so old that it lacked automatic windows—and forced the window down. The glass was covered in dirt and grime, and the valet man coughed as some of it blew up into his face.

He straightened once he'd collected himself. "The service entrance is around back," he told us through pursed lips. "Pull out of the drive, make the first right down the alley, and then turn right again. You won't miss it."

"We're not delivering anything to the hotel." Sage shot him a winning smile, her teeth glistening in the light. "We're going to be staying here."

The man peered into the truck. His eyes first went to me, and then to Noah. We hadn't stopped to change after the fight with the coyotes—we couldn't risk stopping in case whoever was tracking us was still on our tail—so our clothes were dirty and torn.

We probably looked like three homeless people who were living out of this ancient truck.

He studied us for a few seconds and then gently cleared his throat, returning his focus to Sage. "Have you stayed at the Ritz-Carlton before, ma'am?" he asked, a hint of pity in his eyes.

"I have." She reached for her wallet and pulled out a black credit card—one with "The Ritz-Carlton Rewards" written on the front—and flashed it to the valet. "So often, in fact, that I'm a rewards member. And I *really* hope there's a suite available on club level. I love the daily food presentations there. The cheese platters are absolutely divine, don't you think?"

The valet looked shocked as he saw the card and listened to Sage's knowledge of the hotel chain. "Apologies for the confusion Ms..." He paused as he looked at the name on the card. "Ms. Montgomery. Welcome to the Ritz-Carlton, New Orleans." He opened the door for her, making a slight face as his gloved hand touched the dirty handle, and motioned for his colleagues to get the doors for Noah and me. They did. "I'll retrieve a cart for your luggage."

"A luggage cart would be great, but we'll handle our bags ourselves," Sage said as she got out of the truck, shaking out her long hair in a display that caught the eyes of every man within viewing distance.

Well, every man except for Noah, since he was looking straight at me.

My cheeks heated, and I looked away, fidgeting with discomfort as I looked up at the glamorous entrance of the hotel.

"Are you sure?" the valet asked. "It won't be any trouble for the bellman to get your bags."

"We have some precious cargo that I don't trust with anyone but ourselves." Sage reached into the back of the truck and easily lifted the largest of the bags out and up over her head, leaving no room for debate. The bellman rushed a cart over to her, and she lowered it down easily.

Noah reached into the backseat for the bag full of potions, handling it with extra care. He waited until all the other bags were on the cart before placing it on top.

"Oh, and please forgive our appearances." Sage motioned to her clothes before handing the key to the valet. "You see, we stopped by for a bit of paintball on the way here. There's this great place for it just outside the city... what's it called?" She tapped her foot on the ground and looked up out of the corner of her eye, as if trying to remember the name.

"I'm afraid I don't know." The man sounded much

warmer now that Sage had provided an explanation for our messy state—and that he could now rationalize that the red stains on our clothing were paint and not blood.

Ignorance was bliss, right?

"No worries," Sage said. "But it was quite a bit of fun. My friends here won't admit it, but I totally beat both of them." She looked over at me and stuck her tongue out, as if giving me a hard time for being a sore loser.

I rolled my eyes at the ridiculousness of all of this, which I thought was as good of a response as any.

"I'll take your word on that," he said. "Anyway, I'm sure you're eager to get to your suite and clean up."

"Yes." Sage led the way through the entrance of the hotel, holding herself like she was a princess entering a ball instead of a wolf shifter who'd just fought a pack of coyotes. "We certainly do."

RAVEN

*S*age hadn't been kidding about wanting a suite.

Actually, calling this hotel room a "suite" was doing it a disservice. It was more like a glamorous penthouse apartment designed for the Queen of England herself. There was a marble foyer entry, a dining room, a living room with a grand fireplace and billiards table, and a private rooftop terrace that looked out toward the water.

I'd say I couldn't imagine how much it cost, but that wasn't true. Because I'd heard the lady at the front desk when Sage made the reservation.

The suite cost five thousand dollars a night.

And despite all the space in the suite, there was only one bedroom.

"The hotel doesn't have any two bedroom suites." Sage joined me in the doorway, apparently noticing my worried expression. "You and I can share the bed. Noah will take the sofa bed in the living room, as always." She grinned as he set his bag next to the couch.

"Do you two always share a room while hunting?" I asked.

Sage had told me her relationship with Noah was more like siblings than anything else. So with all the money she had, I didn't understand why they wouldn't get two separate rooms.

"Another rule of demon hunting," Noah spoke up from the living room, where he was pacing around examining every corner as if checking to see if the suite was bugged. "Stick with your pack—or partner—as much as possible. There are times on a hunt when it's wise to split up, but sleeping isn't one of them. It's always safer together than apart. *Especially* for those who don't know how to fight."

It didn't take a genius to figure out that he was referring to me.

"Got it." I looked around, not wanting to give him the satisfaction of letting him know that he was irritating me again. "No sleeping alone. But it's safe to go in the bathroom by myself to shower. Right?"

He clenched his fists—I couldn't imagine what I'd

said to anger him so much—and his gaze flared with heat. "Of course it's safe," he said tightly. "In fact, that's the first good idea you've had all day." The fire in his eyes disappeared, replaced with disgust as he lifted his upper lip in a small snarl. "Especially since you stink of coyote."

"At least it's better than smelling like dog." I flung my hair over my shoulder and sauntered to the bathroom, relieved to finally get a moment to myself once I shut the door behind me.

RAVEN

*E*very inch of the huge bathroom was lined with marble, and in the center there was a Jacuzzi tub begging to be filled up for a long, relaxing bath.

I was tempted to do just that. But as I was reaching for the handle, I stopped myself. Because we were on a hunt for demons, which meant despite staying at a luxury hotel, we didn't have time to relax and pamper ourselves. Sage and Noah needed to shower after me. Then we could get started on the reason why we were here—to find and hunt down another demon so Noah could add its tooth to his collection.

I settled for the shower, which in its defense, was incredibly soothing itself. With the water running over my hair, it was easy to close my eyes and pretend I was home, getting ready for class instead of being in a fancy hotel room with two wolf shifters getting ready to hunt a demon.

But the illusion didn't last long. As much as I wanted to stand under the water forever, I had to face what was next. So I turned off the shower and dried off, wrapping myself in a soft, warm towel.

As I was rubbing the fog off the mirror, I realized I hadn't brought any clothes into the bathroom to change into. I'd been so focused on getting some space from Noah that I hadn't thought that far ahead.

Now I was going to have to walk out there in nothing but a towel—albeit, an incredibly cozy, fluffy towel. But it was still a towel, and one that left less to the imagination than any dress I owned.

My face flushed with the thought of it.

I had no intention of prancing in front of Noah in a towel. I didn't want to risk him possibly checking me out. Not that I *minded* the thought of him checking me out—who minded an incredibly hot guy checking them out? But because nothing could ever come of it, since Noah could never imprint or mate with a human.

There was no point in hoping for something that could never be. *Especially* since it seemed clear that while Noah had flirted with me back at the pool house, he'd never been truly interested in me. He'd been attracted to me and had been trying to see how far he could push it—that was all. Flirting with me had just been a game to him.

It *must* have been a game, since from the way he talked to me, he clearly didn't like humans in general. He certainly wouldn't ever be romantically interested in one.

He was just as unavailable to me as a guy with a girlfriend. So that was how I'd think of him.

As a guy with a girlfriend.

So there was no chance I was going to walk in front of him in this towel.

I took a deep breath and stared at myself in the mirror. *You've got this*, I told myself. *Be cool.*

I'd never been stereotypically "cool," but hey, no time to start like the present.

I opened the bathroom door a smidge and peeked out, glad to see that neither Sage nor Noah were in the bedroom section of the suite. Unfortunately, my bag full of clothes that Sage had loaned me wasn't there, either.

"Hey Sage?" I called out, pretty sure she'd be able to hear me. Yes, the suite was big, but wolves had enhanced hearing.

"Yeah?" Her voice echoed out from the living room.

I released the breath I'd been holding. Crisis averted.

"Can you bring my bag to the bedroom so I can change?" I asked.

"Of course." She was through the door in record speed, holding my bag like it was as light as a pillow and placing it on the luggage rack. "Once you're changed, come into the living room," she said. "Because while you were showering, I got in contact with the most powerful witch circle in New Orleans."

RAVEN

I threw on a tank top and a pair of yoga pants and hurried back into the living room. Both Noah and Sage were waiting for me, sitting in chairs around the unlit fireplace.

Noah's eyes went to mine, and I couldn't help it—I froze under his gaze.

Why did he have such a strong effect on me? It made no sense, since he wasn't even nice to me. I felt so stupid for liking him. I was like a grade school girl with a crush on the boy who pulled her hair each time she walked by his desk. And the more time I spent around him, the more that crush seemed to grow.

I needed to put a lid on these emotions—quickly. If I didn't, they were going to get me into serious trouble.

"Leave enough hot water for the rest of us?" he asked, eyeing me up from head to toe.

It was a good thing I was wearing pajamas. Because if he'd looked at me like that while I was in that towel, my face would have turned as red as a tomato.

"Be grateful I took a shower and not a bath," I shot back as I walked over to the couch and made myself comfortable. "Because that Jacuzzi was *mighty* tempting."

Sage huffed and glared at both of us. "Are you two going to be like this for the entire trip?" she asked.

"No," Noah and I said in unison.

I crossed my arms and looked away from him.

"If only I believed you," she muttered.

"Anyway." I sat straighter, eager to change the subject. "What's the story on the witch circle here?"

"As you know, witches can only track something to an exact location if they're close enough to what they're tracking," Sage said, seeming as eager to get to the point as I. "When Amber did the demon tracking spell in LA, she located a demon in New Orleans, but she couldn't pinpoint where that demon was. To do that, she'd have to be in New Orleans herself. That clearly isn't an option, so she gave us the number of a witch contact nearby."

"Did Amber used to come with you on your hunts?" I asked.

"You mean before Azazel murdered Amber's sister so he could force her to track your mom's location for him to kidnap her?" Noah asked.

"Yeah," I said, my voice clipped. I hated the reminder of Azazel and what he'd done. "That's exactly what I mean."

"No." He clenched his fist, as if holding an imaginary blade. "Sage and I hunt alone. At least, before you came along—"

"And ruined everything for you," I continued before he had a chance, rolling my eyes to show how tiring these constant reminders were getting. "I know, I know."

"That wasn't what I was going to say," he said.

"Really?" I eyed him up, not believing him for a second. "Then what *were* you going to say?"

He smirked, looking way too self satisfied for his own good. "You'll never know now, will you?"

It took all of my self-control not to stand up and storm back to the bedroom. Luckily, I was able to rein it in. Saving my mom was worth putting up with Noah's instigating.

"Oh my God." Sage pulled at her hair and leaned back into the sofa, flopping her arms down beside her. "Do you want to hear about the witch or not?"

"Yes," Noah and I said together again.

I glared at him out of the side of my eye. The way we were saying things at the same time was getting seriously annoying.

If I didn't know any better, I'd think it was a sign we were on the same wavelength or whatever.

Good thing I knew better.

"All right." Sage looked back and forth between Noah and me like we'd both grown second heads. I couldn't blame her, since that was what—the *third* time we'd said something at the same time in the past day? But she cleared her throat and continued without mentioning it. "The most powerful witch in New Orleans goes by the name 'The Voodoo Queen,'" she said. "Amber wouldn't tell me her real name—just that we're to address her with her official title."

"Seriously?" I raised an eyebrow. I couldn't picture myself addressing *anyone* like that without laughing.

"Seriously," Sage said. "Some supernaturals can be a bit... eccentric. Especially the witches."

"*Mostly* the witches," Noah added.

"Anyway," Sage continued. "The Voodoo Queen and the witches in her circle work nearby at the Voodoo Queen Store. They use the store as a front for their business of selling both light and dark magic to the supernaturals of New Orleans."

"Great." Noah sat forward and fidgeted in place, looking ready to get moving. "So we'll head there now?"

"I thought you wanted to shower first?" I asked. "Or were you just goading me with that comment about the hot water?"

"Don't get so riled up, Princess," he said. "We don't *have* to rush. I just thought you wanted to finish up this hunt as quickly as possible."

I glared at his sarcastic endearment—I was so *not* the princess type. "You know I do," I said.

He nodded in response, his gaze not leaving mine. There was something about the way he was looking at me… like he truly *cared*.

I shook the thought out of my mind and looked away. Noah didn't care about me. I was just an annoyance to him. Whatever I thought I saw, I was clearly imagining it.

"I'd be up for leaving now," Sage said, breaking the tension between Noah and me. It was a good thing she was here—the two of us would have been a mess without her. "But the Voodoo Queen doesn't start working until after sunset. So Raven's right—we should use this time to freshen up and get some sleep."

I wanted to say that I wasn't tired—I was too wound up to sleep—but I held my tongue. Because Noah's first rule of demon hunting flashed through my mind. The one he'd told me when we were back at the pool house, right after he'd let me join his hunt.

When there's an opportunity to sleep, take it.

Because you never knew when your next chance to sleep would be.

FLINT

Getting Sage back home was going to take longer than anticipated. So I had no choice—I had to talk to Azazel.

Like the other times I'd spoken with the greater demon, we met in an abandoned warehouse in East LA. This wasn't the location of his lair—that was elsewhere. Given his ability to teleport, his lair could be anywhere in the world.

He wouldn't reveal its location until the blood binding ceremony was complete.

Mara was there too, standing by my side. She wore a long red dress, her blonde hair flowing over her shoulders.

Azazel liked Mara to be present whenever we spoke.

It was like he didn't want me to lose sight of what I stood to lose if I didn't follow through on my word.

"I need more time," I said after telling him that Sage had gotten away. "I underestimated my sister, but I won't make the same mistake twice."

Azazel simply stared at me, his red eyes darkening.

I was never scared by anything, but I had to admit— the first time I saw the red eyes of a demon, I was scared.

That changed the moment I imprinted on Mara.

How could I be scared of eyes so similar to those of the woman I loved?

"You never told me why your sister left town." Azazel finally broke the silence between us. "At first, I didn't think much of it—I have more important concerns—but now you have me curious. So tell me, Flint." He stepped forward and brought his hands together, cracking all his knuckles at once. The popping sounds were like nails on a chalkboard to my sensitive shifter hearing, but I held my breath and stopped myself from flinching. "Why did your sister leave this city, and who is she traveling with that's strong enough to help her fight off a pack of coyotes with a mountain lion dyad?"

I swallowed, glad I'd already thought of a cover story for Sage. After all, I certainly couldn't tell Azazel that she was helping Noah—the First Prophet of the wolves of the Vale—on his demon hunting quest. The demons thought Noah had died in the war at the Vale—the war where the Hell Gate had been opened and the demons had burst onto Earth. If Azazel knew Noah was alive, and that my sister was helping him kill demons to steal their teeth for entrance to Avalon... well, I doubted he would take too kindly to Sage, blood binding ceremony or not.

"She imprinted with a wolf from a rival pack." I scrunched my nose as if something smelled bad and added the appropriate amount of annoyance to my tone. It wasn't tough to muster up. Because if this story were true, it wouldn't have been the first time that Sage had tried to get involved with someone that I—her older brother, and more importantly, her *alpha*—didn't approve of. "She hasn't mated with him yet—I doubt she would defy me that greatly. But she's run off with him to prove a point. I underestimated her and her companion against the coyotes, but I won't repeat that mistake. They've stopped over in New Orleans for a few nights, but once they leave, I'll get her back home and have that mutt she's shacking up with taken care of."

Azazel paused and tilted his head, the corner of his lip twitching into a slight smile. Was he... amused? "I don't know, Flint," he finally said. "This sister of yours sounds like more trouble than she's worth."

"His sister is strong." Mara stepped up, her eyes level with Azazel's. "Isn't strength exactly what you desire from your shifter followers?"

"Mara is correct." I took her hand and pulled her to my side, letting her know I could take it from here. "Sage fighting off those coyotes with their mountain lion dyad shows her strength. She's also smart and relentless. She's exactly the type of ally you'll want in the years to come."

Azazel said nothing, and I held my breath, terrified he wouldn't be patient enough to wait for me to retrieve Sage.

What would I do if that were the case?

I couldn't desert my sister. But I also couldn't give up my future with Mara.

He had to give me more time. He just *had* to.

"It certainly sounds like your sister has qualities I'm searching for," he said, and I relaxed slightly, able to breathe once more. But only slightly, since he hadn't voiced his decision yet. "If this shifter she's imprinted on is anything like her—which from what you said, he is— it sounds like he's what I'm looking for, too. So why have him 'taken care of?' Why not bring him here and give your sister similar terms to those I'm giving you with Mara?"

He didn't need to spell it out for me to understand what he meant. The term he had for me and Mara was that he'd only permit us to mate once the blood binding ceremony was complete. I hated that he had the power to *permit* me to do anything—I was an alpha, for crying out loud. My instinct was to simply *take* Mara as my mate and call it a day. With her consent, of course— which I knew I had.

But this was war. If I gave into my instinct to mate with Mara now, Azazel would surely kill me *and* my pack. I needed to do whatever it took to keep us safe from the demons. If that meant allying with them and submitting to Azazel, then so be it. Plus, I'd have Mara in the end. So it wasn't so bad.

Now Azazel wanted the same terms with Sage and this imaginary man she'd imprinted on.

The problem was that she'd never imprinted on Noah—she never had and never would. And if I knew anything about the First Prophet of the Vale, he'd rather die than enter into a blood binding ceremony with the very creatures he was trying to kill.

"That's not a bad idea, Your Grace," I said. That was how Azazel insisted I address him—as *Your Grace*. It went against my instinct as an alpha to defer to anyone in such a way, but I went along with it for Mara. "But I had an idea that I'm sure you'll appreciate even more." I lowered my eyes after speaking, not wanting Azazel to think I was going against him in any way.

"Really?" Azazel stepped forward, looking ready to strangle me if my suggestion disappointed him. "What, exactly, is that?"

I gazed back up at him, making sure to look as determined as I felt. "My sister deserves better than the mutt she's imprinted on," I said. Again, I put the appropriate amount of disgust into my tone. Then I turned to Mara and smiled, not having to fake anything when I looked at my beautiful demon. The desire I felt toward her was real, and I knew it shined in my eyes when I refocused on Azazel. "Which is why I'm hoping she'll imprint on a demon."

Azazel blinked, clearly taken aback by my response. But he got ahold of himself so quickly that someone without enhanced senses wouldn't have noticed. "I understand why you'd want your sister to mate with a demon," he said slowly. "We are, after all, the superior race. But it hasn't slipped my notice that since Mara imprinted on you, she's become emotionally weaker. I tolerate it because the alliance with the Montgomery shifters will add to my numbers, and you promised to go through with the blood binding ceremony if I allow her to mate with you afterward. But how will it help me if *another* one of my demons imprints and mates with a shifter? Because from where I'm standing, I fail to see how it would."

His point was legitimate.

"You're fair to ask such a thing," I said, stalling as I came up with a response that might make sense. Luckily, it came to me a moment later. Because I understood his goal. Kill the supernaturals who don't bind themselves to the demons, and take what remains of the human race as slaves.

I could make his goals and my goals align. I *had* to. It was the only way to make sure Sage remained alive and safe.

"As you said, the other supernaturals on Earth outnumber the demons," I said. "You need this alliance—and alliances from other supernaturals as well. That way you can be confident that once you strike against the supernaturals standing against you, you'll crush them. If the shifter community catches word that not just one of our kind, but *two* of us have imprinted and mated with demons, they'll be more willing to open their minds to the possibility that they might imprint on one, too. And like you said, demons are the superior race." The words tasted like acid when I spoke them, but feeding Azazel's ego was necessary right now. "Once the other packs know that Sage and I have mated with demons and have therefore allied with the strongest force on the planet, they'll be more than eager to follow in the Montgomery pack's footsteps," I concluded. "And isn't that exactly what you want? More shifters to join your cause?"

Azazel stared me down for the longest few seconds of my life. Then the corner of his lip pulled up into a small smile, and I knew I'd succeeded in convincing him to see things my way.

"I do like the sound of that." Azazel stepped forward, his eyes locked on mine in challenge. "But there's one big hole in your plan."

"What's that?" I asked.

"How can you be so sure that your sister will imprint on a demon?"

"My sister and I are of the same blood." I stood straighter, puffing out my chest in pride. "If any other shifter has the chance of imprinting on a demon, it's her."

"All right," Azazel said.

His words shocked me—I hadn't expected it to be that easy. But I stopped myself from showing my surprise. "Really?" I asked.

"You have a fortnight," he said. "Get your sister back

by then. If you can't, we'll proceed with the blood binding ceremony without her."

Azazel teleported out of the warehouse without another word, leaving me staring at the empty spot where he'd just stood—and more determined to get Sage back to LA than ever.

"*T*hat went well," Mara said once Azazel was gone. "All things considering."

"It did." I pulled her toward me and crushed my lips to hers, unable to resist her now that the two of us were alone. I lost myself in her kiss for minutes. She tasted like she smelled—like a warm campfire on a winter night. Like a marshmallow you pull out of the flame at the perfect second, so it's golden, crisp, and sweet. I didn't want to ever let her go.

When we finally broke apart, both of us were breathless.

"I think I know why we were able to imprint on each other, despite being different species," she whispered, her lips still tantalizingly close to mine.

"Really?" I traced my finger over her cheek, barely able to focus with her so near. "And why's that?"

"I think it's because we both have demon blood in us."

"What?" I pulled back in confusion. "I don't have any demon blood in me."

"Yes you do…" She spoke slowly, her eyes lowered as if she thought she'd spoken too soon. "All shifters do."

"I have no idea what you're talking about," I repeated. "Shifters have shifter blood. Not demon blood."

"Shifters have demon blood," she said. "You should know this. Unless…" She paused and bit her lip, looking unsure if she should continue. Her lips were so red and plump—especially when she bit the lower one like that. I wanted to take her as mine right then and there.

But even the desire pulsing through my body for my future mate couldn't distract me from the shocking revelation she'd just dumped on me.

"Go on," I said, breathing steadily to calm myself. 'Whatever you have to say, I can take it."

"I know you can," she said. "I didn't mean to imply you couldn't. I'm just surprised, because it sounds like you don't know how shifters were created in the first place."

"Shifters have existed for thousands of years," I said.

"We're natural creatures of Earth, unlike the vampires, witches, and even the Nephilim. We belong here. We always have, and we always will."

"No," she said. "Shifters aren't natural creatures of the Earth. If anything, you're most similar to the Nephilim. Because the Nephilim were created by drinking angel blood from the Holy Grail... and the shifters were created from drinking demon blood from the Dark Grail."

"Explain." I blinked, unsure I heard right.

"Which part?" She gazed up at me, her crimson eyes swirling with knowledge—knowledge that only a creature born centuries ago could have.

My future mate was truly extraordinary.

"The Grails," I said, unable to hide my disbelief as I spoke. "You're saying that that *Holy Grail* actually exists?"

"Oh, it exists," she said with a knowing smile. "It's the Holy Cup that the angels used to create the first Nephilim. And like all the four major holy objects, it has a dark counterpart. The Dark Grail."

"Which you're saying was used to create the shifters," I said, the possibility still not completely sinking in. Because if this was true, it meant everything I'd always thought I'd known about myself—about my species—was a lie.

"I'm not 'just saying' it," she said. "It's a fact. All demons know about the Dark objects. Just as all Nephilim knew about the Holy objects. Or *knew* about them, before the Nephilim were wiped out."

"And where's this Dark Grail now?" I asked.

"Locked somewhere in Hell." She shrugged. "Just like the Holy Grail was locked in Heaven."

"Hm." I glanced around the warehouse, unwilling to simply *accept* this. I believed that *Mara* believed the Grails existed. But they sounded more like items of legend to me than anything else.

So I returned my focus to what she'd previously said —that shifters were created by demons, and therefore had demon blood. It was a jarring thought, since it went against everything I ever knew. But I also knew that Mara wouldn't lie to me.

"Up until you and me, shifters could only imprint on other shifters," I said, still trying to make sense of this shocking revelation. "But if it's true that shifters have demon blood, it could explain why we were able to imprint on each other."

"It's just a theory," she said. "Shifters were created from mixing demon blood with human blood. So technically, it doesn't seem *too* out there for that to explain our imprint."

"If that's true, than shifters should be able to imprint

on humans, too," I said. "And *that's* certainly never happened."

"Are you sure about that?" She raised an eyebrow.

"Yes." I held her gaze. "I'm sure."

"I believe you," she said. "Maybe it's only demons you can also imprint with. Or maybe something changed when the Hell Gate was opened. Or maybe this is something unique just to us. Who knows?" Her wide eyes looked so confused and innocent, igniting a fire in me that I couldn't ignore.

"I certainly don't." I stepped forward, taking her in my arms again. I could only resist her for so long. Even though I couldn't make love to her—that would complete the mating process, which Azazel had forbidden until the binding ceremony was complete—there were many other ways we could satisfy our desire for one another until then. "All I know is that you're mine, and nothing in this world or any other world is ever going to change that." I slid my fingers through the slit of her dress and trailed them up the inside of her thigh, teasing her.

She arched into me and moaned my name, and I knew that the talking was done for now. I'd contemplate everything she'd told me—and what it meant about who I was—later.

For now, I crushed my lips to hers and pinned her against the nearest wall, eager for the day when the blood binding ceremony would be complete and I could finally make her mine for good.

Sage's alarm went off an hour before sunset, waking us up from our naps. Even though I hadn't thought I was tired earlier, I'd fallen asleep the moment I'd gotten under the covers.

We changed and got ready for a night in the French Quarter, since Sage had told me it was important to blend in. Which meant looking the part of tourists out for a night in New Orleans—hair, makeup, and all. The whole getting ready process reminded me of when my friends and I got ready to go out back home. The only difference from the way I normally dressed was that instead of wearing heels or flats, I was wearing the black combat boots Sage had given me.

After all, I needed a place to keep my knife. Which was yet another present from Sage. Unlike Noah, at least she thought I was somewhat capable of defending myself.

When we left the bedroom, we found Noah in the living room pulling on a shirt. I couldn't help but check out his abs—they were flat and perfectly chiseled. The only way I could have stopped myself from looking was if I'd been blind.

"Took you girls long enough to get ready." He glanced over at us, his eyes stopping when he looked at me. He roamed over every bit of me—from my head to my toes—and I could have sworn he'd stopped breathing there for a second.

"What?" I shifted on my feet, wishing he would stop looking at me that way. He was giving me mixed signals, and I didn't like it.

"You can't go out dressed like that," he said.

"Why not?" I placed my hands on my hips, annoyed and unwilling to back down. "I'm not dressed any differently than Sage."

"Sage knows how to take care of herself," he said. "With you dressed like that, you'll only bring more attention to yourself. Don't make us babysit you more than we already have to."

"I'm wearing shorts and a tank top," I pointed out. "I'll hardly be the most dressed up person out tonight. It's not like I'm wearing a tight sequin dress or something else that's begging for attention."

His eyes traveled up my bare legs again. When his gaze finally met mine, his pupils were wide and dilated.

If I didn't know any better, I'd think he was more worried about *himself* being distracted by what I was wearing—not about my bringing unwanted attention to myself like he'd claimed.

"Go change into jeans." He reached for his weapons belt and slung it around his hips. "We have a few minutes to spare."

"It's hot out," I said. "I'll be more comfortable in shorts." I narrowed my eyes at him—I *hated* being told what to wear. But I also didn't want to not listen to him and risk jeopardizing our mission.

So I turned to Sage for a voice of reason.

"What do you think?" I asked her. "Am I okay in this, or do you think it'll be safer if I change?"

"You're absolutely fine in what you're wearing," she said, and then she turned to Noah, looking as irritated by him as I felt. "You need to cool it, all right? I get that you're stressed. But giving Raven a hard time about everything she does won't help our mission."

"It's not my fault that she's completely unprepared for what she's about to walk into," he said.

"I'm not *completely* unprepared," I said. "Sage gave me

that knife and taught me about potions. And I have both of you to protect me. So I should be good, right?"

"Only because you have us to protect you," Noah said.

I sighed in frustration, knowing that I shouldn't have expected him to say anything else.

"Let's just go." Sage strutted toward the door, not looking back at us. "There's no point in the two of you standing here bickering when we have a Voodoo Queen to meet."

RAVEN

Both our hotel and the Voodoo Queen store were in the French Quarter, so we only had to walk a few blocks before arriving. Even though the sun was still setting, the streets of New Orleans were abuzz with lively jazz music and people partying at the bars.

We approached a red brick building on the corner and saw the hanging sign for the Voodoo Queen store. The place looked eccentric, to say the least. Shuttered windows with peeling black paint displayed a crowded selection of beads, dream catchers, and painted skulls.

I could already tell that this store was going to be *very* different from Tarotology, the relaxed new age shop my mom owned in Venice Beach.

The inside of the store was packed—mostly with tourists in khakis and t-shirts who must have only been there for souvenirs. I doubted most of them even knew how to read a tarot deck. Every inch of wall and surface space was covered in more masks, beads, and artwork than one person could possibly sift through. Even the ceiling was dripping with hanging objects.

My eyes stopped on an illuminated glass display inside the counter, which was full of tarot decks. Finally, something I recognized.

The woman working the counter was too busy ringing up customers to glance in our direction. But at the sight of the tarot decks, I remembered the eerily accurate tarot reading both my mom and I had drawn for me before she'd been abducted.

The reading said my entire world was about to change in a moment of sudden upheaval, and that I was about to go on an important journey where I'd need to take charge if I wanted to succeed.

My tarot deck was still in my apartment, just like everything else I owned. I'd had to make a split second decision to go with Noah and Sage to try saving my mom, and I hadn't exactly had time to stop and pack.

I'd never believed in the cards. But seeing them now, I wanted to buy a deck to have with me on this journey.

Given the fact that an entire supernatural world that I'd never known about existed right beside my own, it no longer seemed so far fetched to believe that tarot readings could be real, too. Maybe I could even do readings to help us on our hunt.

I was about to voice this desire to Noah and Sage when Noah removed his cloaking ring from his finger and handed it to me.

"Hold this for a minute." He placed it in my hand so quickly that I had no choice but to do as he said.

Suddenly, a regal black woman in a long purple dress stepped out of the shadows and approached Noah, her head held high as she eyed him up. She wore an intricately feathered headdress that while beautiful, must have been sweltering in the heat. "You're new in town." She said it as a statement, not a question. "What brings you to the store?"

"Just passing through," he said simply. "We're here to meet with the Voodoo Queen."

The corners of her lips twitched slightly upward at the mention of the Voodoo Queen. "I can take *you* to the back room for a consultation," she replied, speaking only to Noah. "Your companions will wait here."

He stood straighter—the woman was so tall that including her headdress, the two of them were the same height. "There's no need to hide anything from my companions," he said. "They go where I go."

She took a deep breath and glanced at us as if we held no importance whatsoever. Then she returned her focus to Noah. "Very well," she said, turning to the back of the shop and raising her skirt to walk. "Follow me."

RAVEN

*S*he led us through the back curtain and opened the door to a room that reminded me of the apothecary that Amber and the LA witches had in their Beverly Hills mansion. It had a table in the center, and the shelves along the walls were full of potions, crystals, pendulums, candles, and the like.

The woman removed her headdress, placed it on a counter, and turned to face us. "A shifter and two humans." She eyed up Sage and me suspiciously, as if we didn't belong here. "This is most unusual. Why did you come to me tonight?"

Sage removed her ring and handed it to me as well. "As Noah said when we arrived, we've come to speak with the Voodoo Queen."

"Then you've come to the right place." The

woman smiled. "Because I *am* the Voodoo Queen. And I must say, that's quite the expensive magic you have there." She glanced at the two cloaking rings in my hand. "I take it that all three of you are shifters?"

"They're both shifters," I said. "I'm a human."

"Interesting." She pursed her lips, as if trying to figure the three of us out. "Of course, I'd never turn down paying customers—especially those able to afford such strong magic. But I must say that you've piqued my curiosity. How did a human come to be traveling with two strong wolf shifters?"

"It's a long story." Noah stepped closer to me, as if staking his territory. "But you can trust Raven. She's under our protection."

"I see that," she said. "And don't worry, young wolf. I won't harm your girlfriend."

Noah and I rushed to deny that I was his girlfriend at the exact same time, speaking over each other in the process.

"Calm down." The Voodoo Queen chuckled, holding a hand up for us to stop talking. "Your relationship is hardly as important to me as how you got here. And despite it being a long story, I'd like to hear it—and I'd like to hear it from Raven." She motioned to me as she said the last part.

"We're on a time sensitive mission," Sage cut in. "If you don't mind, it's best if we just get to the point—"

"Do you want me to help you or not?" The Voodoo Queen crossed her arms and raised an eyebrow.

She had a serious diva attitude, and I liked it.

"Yes," I answered before Noah or Sage had a chance.

"That's what I thought." She smiled and turned to me. "So please, tell me your story."

I glanced at Noah and Sage. I wanted to do as the Voodoo Queen asked, but not without their permission. After all, while my instincts told me to trust the Voodoo Queen, I needed to make sure they agreed.

Noah nodded, and Sage smiled, which I took as a cue to go on.

And so, I went back to the very beginning and told her everything.

RAVEN

I started from the night of my twenty-first birthday and went from there. Getting attacked by a demon behind the restaurant at the Santa Monica Pier, Noah and Sage saving my life, coming home to find my mom had been abducted, speaking with Rosella to learn that I had to go to Avalon to save my mom, and officially joining Noah's hunt.

Finally I reached the present, where the three of us had won the fight against the coyotes, arrived to New Orleans, and come to her store.

"We're here for two reasons," Noah took over once I'd finished. "A cloaking ring for Raven, and a scrying spell to locate the demon in New Orleans."

"It's an interesting story indeed." The Voodoo Queen

tapped her long fingernails along the top of the table, as if she were deciding whether or not she wanted to help us or not. "The scrying spell is light magic that I can perform for you now. But the cloaking ring is dark magic that will take more time. One of the witches in my circle can have it ready for you to pick up tomorrow evening."

"Perfect," Sage said. "We'll take both. How much?"

"Since your story was so entertaining, I'll give you a deal," the Voodoo Queen said. "One hundred thousand for both the cloaking ring and the scrying spell, and I'll also throw in a simple cloaking potion for free for Raven to drink right now. The potion will last until the ring is ready tomorrow."

"One hundred thousand *dollars?*" I widened my eyes, sure I must have misunderstood.

"Creating the ring will require dark magic," she replied. "Witches must pay the price to perform dark magic. It's only fair that our customers pay the price, too."

"What type of 'price' do you have to pay to perform dark magic?" I had a feeling that I didn't want to know the answer, but that didn't stop me from asking anyway. I'd always been too curious for my own good.

She stared me down, her expression unreadable.

"Each time a dark magic spell is performed, the witch must take a life." Her eyes flashed with darkness, and a shiver ran up my spine. "Eventually, a witch who performs enough dark magic will lose the ability to perform light magic. It's not something that any of our kind views casually."

"So to create a cloaking ring for me, you have to *kill* someone?" I backed up, not liking the sound of this.

"Not me," she said. "I perform light magic, so I won't be creating your ring. But yes—when one of my sisters creates your cloaking ring, she'll have to make a blood sacrifice to complete the spell."

"No." I handed Noah and Sage's rings back to them, not wanting to touch them now that I knew how the rings had come to be. "If someone has to die for my cloaking ring to be created, then I don't want it."

"Don't be ridiculous." Noah scoffed. "If you don't have the cloaking ring, you could die. We *all* could die."

"You don't know that," I said.

"Someone knows who we are, and they're after us." He held his gaze with mine and crossed his arms, not looking like he was going to back down. "They sent the coyotes after us. Who knows what they'll try next? If we want to live—if you want to save your mom—then you need this ring. No matter what the cost."

"So I'm supposed to do what?" I asked. "Just be okay with the fact that someone had to die so I could live?"

"We have a system in place, dear." The Voodoo Queen spoke gently, her eyes brimming with sympathy as she looked at me. "One of my sisters works at a nearby hospice. She ensures that the lives we take are ones that were about to end, anyway. She releases them from their suffering. They—and their families—are always more at peace once it's done."

"That doesn't make it okay," I said, although it *did* make me feel better than if they were taking the life of someone who had many healthy years ahead of them. It wasn't okay, but at the same time, it wasn't as bad as it could be.

"We know that," she said. "We only sacrifice those in the worst possible conditions—those who are in too much pain to go on living. We wouldn't have it any other way. And we only offer dark magic spells to those who deserve it, like you. That's why I asked to hear your story. And what a story it was. Raven—please believe me when I say that you're worth saving. Your mom is worth saving, too. If you can find out why the demons are abducting humans... then who knows? Maybe whatever you discover will be the key to their defeat."

"You really think so?" I asked, hope rising in my chest as she spoke.

"My intuition tells me that there's something special about you—something that will be extremely important further down the road," she said. "And I always trust my intuition. No matter what."

I nodded and pressed my lips together, saying nothing as I thought it over. It still didn't sit well with me that all dark magic existed because a life had been ended. But my mom was in danger and I was the only one who could save her. Who knew where the demons had brought her, or what they were doing to her? It pained me whenever I thought of it. The police couldn't help her—they knew nothing about the supernatural world. I couldn't go to my grandparents with all of this without them thinking I was crazy. Which meant it was up to me. With the help of Noah and Sage, of course.

And Noah was right—to save my mom, I needed to be alive. So I needed to do everything possible to *stay* alive.

"I'll accept the ring," I finally said. "On one condition."

"What's that?" The Voodoo Queen sat back slightly— she didn't seem like the type of woman who was often given conditions.

"I want to know the name of the person whose life was sacrificed so my cloaking ring could exist," I said. "That way I can pay my respects by sending something to their family in their time of grief." It wasn't much, but it was better than nothing.

The Voodoo Queen paused—for a moment I thought she was going to say no.

"All right." She nodded and held her hand out for me to shake. "You have yourself a deal."

RAVEN

$\mathcal{T}$he Voodoo Queen did a scrying spell for the demon and located him at a bar on Bourbon Street. He was literally less than five minutes away from the store.

Sage paid her with her fancy black credit card, I downed the cloaking potion that would make me untraceable for the next twenty-four hours, and the Voodoo Queen reminded us to pick up the cloaking ring tomorrow evening (as if we'd forget). We said goodbye and headed out.

Now that more time had passed, the streets were more crowded. The music was louder, the dresses were getting slinkier, and the people were looking drunker. And as I looked around the busy crowd, I couldn't deny the nervous energy coursing through every inch of my body.

I wasn't ready for this.

The last time I'd seen a demon—which was the *only* time I'd seen a demon—I was helpless against his strength. Besides the knife hidden in my boot and my new basic knowledge of potions, I was still a human. And yes, I hated how Noah kept talking about my being a human like it was a terrible thing. But now that we were actually on our way to hunt down a demon, I realized he had a point.

Because humans were weaker than supernaturals. *Much* weaker.

The only reason I'd survived the demon attack at the Santa Monica Pier was because Noah and Sage had burst onto the scene and saved me. Without them, I would have been captured or dead.

With the doubt setting in, I walked slower, not sure if I could handle this. But I wasn't going to say anything. I was committed to helping them—I wasn't going to turn back now. I could do this. And if worst came to worst, I trusted Noah and Sage to protect me. They'd done it once, so they could do it again.

"You should go back to the hotel," Noah said, interrupting my train of thought.

"Why?" I jerked my head to look at him. "We have to go hunt that demon."

"Sage and I can handle it." He studied me with what looked like worry in his eyes. "You're nervous, which is understandable. Let us handle this."

"I'm not nervous," I lied.

"You are," he said. "I can smell it."

I frowned and gave a small sniff, even though I couldn't smell anything other than the alcohol and sweat from the people around us.

Stupid supernatural enhanced senses.

"Fine—maybe I'm slightly nervous," I said, since apparently there was no use denying it. "But you were with me at Rosella's. You heard what she said about my future. If I want to pass the Angel Trials—and if I want to save my mom—I have to come with you on your hunts."

"Which is why you're here with us now," he said. "Now, let me walk you back to the hotel. Sage and I will take over from here."

I glared at him, because he couldn't be serious. "I'm pretty sure that when Rosella said I needed to come with you on your hunts, she didn't mean I should sit inside the hotel room while you and Sage kill the demons," I said. "Besides, she wouldn't have told me to go with you if I was going to die at our first stop. So I'm coming with you. End of story."

"The future's never set in stone," Sage said. "Every supernatural in the world knows about Rosella and how her power works. She can see *possibilities*. She can't know for sure which possible future will happen until it comes to pass."

"Are you agreeing with Noah?" I couldn't believe it. Until now, I thought Sage was on my side.

Apparently I was wrong.

"I'm not 'agreeing' with anyone," she said. "I just thought you should know the facts before making a decision."

I knew the facts. I was about to walk into a bar where a known demon was hanging out, waiting to do who knows what to who knows who. He was probably searching for his next victim to kidnap.

The thought of being close to a demon again made my stomach do all kinds of twists and turns.

But Noah and Sage had protected me last time. They'd protect me this time—and all other times to come in the future—as well.

"I need to do this, and I trust both of you to protect me," I said, making sure I sounded as confident as possible. "I'm coming with you."

"Only on one condition," Noah said.

"And what's that?" I raised an eyebrow, amused. Noah had apparently taken a page out of my book after the condition I'd given the Voodoo Queen and was now giving me one in return.

"You have to do everything Sage and I say," he said. "That means if we tell you to stay in one spot and be quiet, you stay in that spot and be quiet. No more attempts at heroics like you did with the coyotes."

"They weren't just coyotes," I reminded him. "One of them was a mountain lion dyad."

"You're avoiding the point," he said. "You said you trust us. If that's true, you need to listen to us and let us protect you. Got it?"

"Got it," I said.

He studied me for a few seconds, looking like he didn't believe me. "I'm not sure you do," he said. "Promise you'll listen to us this time. Say it out loud and convince me that you mean it."

I sighed—I'd already agreed when I said that I got it. Did I really have to spell it out for him that I meant it?

According to the way he was watching me and waiting, yes, I did.

"Why do you even care so much?" I asked. "I would think it would be a relief for you if the weak human you're stuck babysitting did something stupid and got killed. Then you wouldn't have to be held back by me anymore."

He sucked in a sharp breath, as if just the thought of that happening pained him. But his eyes hardened a second later, once more looking like he didn't care at all. "No one's getting killed under my watch," he said. "Except for the demons. So you either make the promise, or you're going back to the hotel. Your call. Just decide quickly, because we don't have all night."

"I promise I'll listen to you this time," I said, holding his gaze so he knew I meant it. "And that I won't do anything that might stop you and Sage from being able to protect me."

"Good." He nodded and reached for his weapons belt, like he was making sure his knife was still there. From the serious way he was watching me, I could tell he was satisfied with my promise. "Let's go."

With that, he turned around and led the way to the bar.

RAVEN

espite Noah's initial urge to lead the way, he eventually let Sage and I take control. Never being taught how to read made him pretty terrible at directions.

It didn't take us long to find the bar—it was the busiest one on Bourbon Street. Even though the night had just begun, there was already a line out the door of people waiting to get in.

We waited in line, and I flashed my ID to the bouncer before being let inside. This was my first time going to a bar since turning twenty-one—the restaurant I'd gone to with my friends on my birthday didn't count, since they let anyone in.

I certainly hadn't expected that the first time I went

to a 21+ bar would be in New Orleans with two wolf shifters on a mission to kill a demon.

My life had seriously taken a turn for the weird.

Inside the bar was packed with partiers, and the music was so loud that I could barely hear. I looked around, expecting a demon to jump out at us at any moment.

Would I even know when the demon was near? Eli had looked like a normal guy when I'd met him at the restaurant on the Pier.

Since the demons looked normal, how did Noah and Sage know where they were? I wanted to ask, but I stopped myself. Because I didn't want to give us away. If the demon was nearby and overheard, then I'd destroy the mission before it had a chance to begin. So I kept my mouth shut.

It was probably something I should have asked beforehand, so I wasn't wondering the moment we stepped into the bar where the demon was hanging out.

I felt stupid for not asking earlier. Then again, I'd learned so much in such a short period of time that I had a lot on my mind. I shouldn't be so hard on myself. All things considering, I thought I was doing a pretty good job handling everything that had been thrown at me recently.

Since Sage and Noah had elevated senses, I assumed

they could smell the demons. Noah had said earlier that I smelled like a human, and he and Sage could smell that the shifter pack that had attacked us was coyotes. It didn't seem far-fetched that they could smell demons, too.

Noah said something to me, but the music was so loud that I couldn't hear him.

"What?" I asked, pressing the inside of my ear in the hopes that it would help me hear him better. It was a trick my friends had told me about when we'd started college.

Noah just reached for my wrist and guided me to the bar in the center of the room. Heat rushed through my veins the moment his skin touched mine, and I wasn't aware of anything but where he was touching me. The energy I felt from his touch was unreal. Somehow, I managed to follow him to the bar without tripping over my own feet.

Once we were there, he found an empty seat and sat me down in it. "Wait here," he said. "Sage and I will go check for our friend."

I assumed by the way he was calling the demon a "friend" that he didn't want to risk the demon possibly overhearing our conversation.

"You want me to sit here *alone?*" I gaped at him, sure my eyes looked like they were popping out of my head.

"You're in the center of the bar, surrounded by people," he said. "As long as you're in plain sight, you're safe. Think back to Santa Monica. Eli didn't try anything until you were alone, right?"

"Right," I said.

He'd waited until I went to the bathroom, and then he'd nabbed me in the empty hallway and pulled me out to the alley behind the restaurant.

"Exactly," he said. "They have no interest in revealing themselves, and they're not stupid. They bring the least attention to themselves as possible. As long as you stay right here, you'll be safe. I'll be checking the ground floor, and I won't lose sight of you the entire time. Sage will go upstairs and check there."

"And you want me to just… sit here?"

"Yep." He reached into his jacket, pulled out a wad of cash, and handed it to me. "Buy yourself a drink. Something non-alcoholic. We can't have you getting drunk on the job."

I glanced down at the money he'd handed over. It was all hundred dollar bills.

Did he have no concept of what this was worth?

"I don't think any drinks at this place are *that* expensive." I plucked one of the bills out, shoved it into my pocket, and handed the rest back to him.

"Keep it." He shrugged, not taking it back.

I didn't want to draw attention to the bunch of hundred dollar bills in my hand, so I folded them up and put them in my pocket with the others. "Thanks," I said, suddenly feeling like a sitting target with this much cash on me at once.

"I'll come back once I find our friend," he said. "Until then, stay here." He watched me, clearly waiting for me to confirm that I had no intentions of trying to pull off any "heroics" again.

"I promise." I held out my pinky in a pinky promise.

He looked at my hand like I'd gone nuts, making no move to link his finger with mine. "What are you doing?" he asked.

"It's a pinky promise," I said slowly. "The most serious of all promises?"

He stared at me blankly. Clearly he had no idea what I was talking about.

"Never mind." I dropped my hand down to my side. "Go find our friend. I'll be waiting right here."

He nodded, studying me again as if making sure I was actually going to stay put. Then he walked away to find the demon.

As he walked away, he kept me in his line of vision—making me confident that he'd meant it when he said he'd keep me safe.

RAVEN

*I*t seemed flashy to hand the bartender a hundred dollar bill at a dive bar like this, so I settled for a cup of tap water with a lime. The bartender didn't look pleased that I'd ordered the one free item on the menu. But it wasn't his place to tell me to move, so he placed the drink in front of me, gave me a dirty look that said, "you better buy something that costs money later," and moved on to the next customer.

I was sipping my water, keeping an eye on Noah as he walked around the room, when a guy around my age squeezed into the spot next to me. I assumed he was there to grab a drink—lots of people were trying to grab drinks to bring back to where they were hanging out with their friends. So I scooted over to make room for him, not paying much attention to him.

"You're at the hottest bar in New Orleans and you're sitting by yourself drinking a water?" He looked right at me, clearly speaking to me.

I was taken aback—I hadn't expected anyone to try talking to me. The guy was my typical "type." He had brown, boy-band styled hair and was wearing a light plaid shirt. He looked nice enough. If it had been any other circumstance, I would have been happy to chat with him and see if we clicked.

Now I was just annoyed that he was blocking my view of Noah.

But he was waiting for me to answer, so I needed to say something—anything other than the truth.

"I'm just waiting for some friends," I said the first thing that popped into my mind. After all, it wasn't a lie. I *was* waiting for some friends.

I was waiting for them to locate a demon in the bar so we could kill him and pocket one of his teeth.

"How about a drink while you wait?" he asked. "A *real* drink." His eyes flashed with amusement as he glanced at my water again.

There was nothing strange about his comment—it was perfectly normal for a guy to offer to buy a girl a drink at a bar—but something about him made the back of my neck tingle in warning.

"No, thanks." I scanned the room, hoping Noah and

Sage would hurry up and locate the demon.

"Are you sure?" he asked. "I hear the margaritas here are fantastic."

"I don't drink." I faced away from him, hoping he'd get the hint.

"Why not?" He reached for my arm. His fingers brushed against my skin, sending more warning shivers down my spine.

I pulled my arm away from his hand and glared at him. "I just don't," I said. "Aren't your friends waiting for you?"

Hint: Leave me alone.

"Nope." He smirked. "They all drank too much during the day. So I had two choices—stay in with a bunch of guys puking their guts out from too many Bloody Marys, or hit up the town by myself. Naturally, I chose choice number two."

"Cool," I said, even though I couldn't care less. I *wanted* to get up and leave this guy at the bar. By staying here, I was giving him the impression that I didn't mind how he kept pressing me to talk to him.

But getting up and going somewhere else would go against my promise to Noah.

While this guy was irritating, I could put up with him if that's what it took to keep my promise that I'd stay where Noah had left me. I hadn't realized that putting up with a pushy frat boy was part of the demon hunting job, but it was better than failing at the first assignment I'd been given. Of course, waiting around at the bar while Noah and Sage scoped out the area wasn't much of an assignment, but I needed to start somewhere. Once I proved that I could do this, hopefully they'd start trusting me more.

"So," he continued, apparently oblivious to the fact that I wasn't interested in chatting with him. "What brings you to New Orleans if you don't drink? If you didn't notice, that's kind of what this city's all about." He held his hands out, motioning to the stumbling, drunken crowd around us.

"I don't mean to be rude," I said. "But I'm really just here to wait for my friends."

He frowned and studied me, his eyes feeling like they were boring into my soul.

That creepy feeling from before amplified by a thousand.

Suddenly, Noah was by my side, wrapping his arm around my waist and pulling me close to him. My breath caught—the warm, electric feeling I had whenever Noah touched me flooding my body.

Noah glared at the frat boy like he was a stray animal who's wandered onto his territory. "Hands off my girl," he said. His voice was calm—deadly and scary.

"Whoa there." The frat boy chuckled and held his hands in the air, although he kept his creepy eyes on me. "You didn't tell me you had a boyfriend."

"I *don't* have a boyfriend." I tried to pull out of Noah's grasp, but he held me tightly in place. I squirmed again, but Noah was strong—I wouldn't be able to move until he wanted me to.

Annoying frat guy or not, this display wasn't necessary. I was handling myself just fine. Didn't Noah have more important things to worry about—like locating the demon?

"Do you know this guy?" The frat guy looked back and forth between Noah and me in concern. I couldn't blame him. Noah looked pretty intimidating in his all-black leather getup. And I had no doubt that I looked panicked.

Before I realized what was happening, Noah leaned down and pressed his lips to mine. My heart leaped, and every bone in my body felt like it was melting into his. I didn't believe this was happening. I couldn't think—all I could do was kiss him back.

A warm, golden light surrounded us, and everything around us ceased to exist. As we kissed, so many emotions coursed through me—desire, happiness, need, and most importantly, the feeling that this was *right*. Strings connected our hearts so they were was beating in time with one another, and our lips moved perfectly in sync, as if we'd kissed each other millions of times before.

Kissing Noah felt like I was coming home.

I felt his soul in that kiss—his burning need to do what was right, and to fix everything he'd destroyed. I didn't even know what that *meant*, but it was what I felt. No—it was what *he* felt. It was like his feelings and my feelings had merged into one. I could feel his undeniable need to protect me and keep me safe, no matter what the cost. If I didn't know any better, I might have even felt love. I knew that was silly, since Noah and I didn't love each other—we didn't even *like* each other. But everything about the way we were holding each other and kissing each other said differently.

When he eventually broke the kiss, I gazed up at him, so many questions racing through my mind at once.

What on Earth had just happened? Why had he done that? How had he made me feel that way? I mean, Noah certainly wasn't the first guy I'd ever kissed... but never once had I ever kissed someone and felt like it wasn't just our lips touching, but our souls as well.

His arms remained around me, as if he never wanted to let me go. And from the dazed way he was staring back down at me, I knew that the intense connection I'd felt while we'd kissed had been mutual.

Before I could get myself together enough to speak, Noah ripped his gaze away from mine and turned back to the frat boy. "She's my girlfriend," he said, his voice huskier than before. "I think that was proof enough." He didn't wait for a response before pulling me off the chair and leading me away from the bar. He clasped his hand in mine, not letting go the entire time.

But I knew that look I'd seen in his eyes.

It was the same look he'd given me whenever I asked a question he didn't want to answer. He was closing himself off—shutting down emotionally.

I refused to let him do that. After a kiss like that, I deserved answers.

"What was that about?" I asked once we were on the opposite side of the room.

He pulled me closer and glanced around the room, his eyes darting around like he was ready to attack at any moment. Finally he refocused on me, although I could tell he was still ready to strike. "I was saving your life," he said, gripping my hand tighter as he spoke.

"From what?" I asked, since his response didn't make any sense. "A frat boy who was trying to buy me a drink?"

"That guy wasn't a frat boy." He laughed, although I could tell he thought it was anything but funny. "He was the demon."

RAVEN

"What?" I balked. "No way. That guy couldn't have been…" I was about to say that he couldn't have been the demon. But I paused mid-sentence, knowing I was wrong.

Because Eli had been a demon. And when I'd met Eli at the restaurant at the Santa Monica Pier, he'd looked like a typical surfer-dude tourist. Nothing about him looked outwardly demonic.

"He was." Noah nodded and lowered his lips to my ear, speaking lower so only I could hear. "You can't see past his glamour. I can. Trust me—he's the target."

I blinked a few times, taking it in.

The knowledge that I'd been so close to the demon—that the demon had *touched* me—erased all the gooey, melty-ness I'd felt from Noah's kiss.

Well, it didn't erase the after effects of his kiss completely. But it certainly dampened it.

I didn't think anything would ever make me forget it completely. Yes, I understood now that Noah was trying to get me away from the demon. But there *had* to have been other ways to go about that.

Ways that didn't involve kissing me with so much love and passion that the entire universe ceased to exist around me.

Noah had wanted to kiss me—I had no doubt about that. Kissing me went against all the boundaries I'd set up between us, but he'd ignored that and done it anyway. I wasn't sure how I felt about that. So I definitely still intended on getting some answers about why he'd done that and if he'd felt the same thing I did—the connection between our souls.

After we killed the demon.

Which meant I needed to box up my feelings for Noah for now and only think about the task at hand. Easier said than done, but I needed to try.

"Where's Sage?" I asked, trying my hardest to get focused again.

"She's still scoping out upstairs," he said.

I glanced upstairs, knowing that Sage wasn't going to find the demon there. Then I glanced back to the bar.

My heart dropped to my feet when I saw that the demon was no longer sitting where we'd left him.

I scanned the area and spotted him heading toward the exit.

"He's leaving." Anxiety clawed at my stomach at the thought of him getting away. "Aren't we going to stop him?"

"*I'm* going to stop him," Noah said. "You're going to wait right here."

He looked at me with such intense determination that I had no choice but to nod that I understood. He must have trusted that I'd listen, because he untangled his fingers from mine and walked toward the demon.

I shook out my hand—I hadn't realized how tightly Noah had been holding it until he let go. It didn't feel like I'd get the circulation back in my fingers for the rest of the night.

Once Noah was about ten feet behind the demon, the demon stopped in his tracks.

He looked at Noah, and then back at me. His eyes were hard, and for a second I could have sworn that I'd seen a glint of red coming off of them. It could have just been the light... but I knew it was more.

Because demons had red eyes. Now that I knew what he was, I must have been seeing the true color of his eyes.

And for some reason, he'd zeroed in on me. Not just now, but earlier at the bar.

He was after me. I didn't know how I knew, but I *knew* just as much as I knew that the kiss between Noah and me had meant something real.

Instead of continuing toward the exit, the demon pivoted and walked toward where the band was playing at the corner nearby.

Noah remained where he was for a few seconds, his eyes still on the demon. Then he headed back to me. He positioned himself with his back to the wall so he could keep watch over the demon and pulled me close to him.

"We can't attack in here," he said, his voice low. "It'll draw too much attention to us and put too many humans at risk. We have to wait until he leaves, follow him out, and launch our attack from there."

"So what do we do until then?" I forced myself to focus on the issue at hand and not on how close Noah's body was to mine. "Just stay here and wait?"

"Yep," he said. "Another rule of demon hunting—it's not fun and games all the time. Sometimes, we have to set up a good, old fashioned stakeout and wait around for the right time to strike."

"Makes sense." I glanced back over at the demon.

Every so often, he would glance back over at me,

although he'd turn back around so quickly that I wouldn't have noticed unless I was already aware of him. And he was definitely looking at me—not at Noah.

Which was when I had a crazy idea.

"I'm going to go upstairs and find Sage," I told Noah. "She needs to be updated on what's happening."

"I can send her a message," he said.

"How?" I asked. "I mean, to send a text, you have to be able to read..." I trailed off, feeling bad about bringing it up. It wasn't Noah's fault that he grew up without being taught how to read or write. He'd have to learn sometime, but obviously hunting down the ten demons was his priority for now.

"We use voice messages." He didn't look at me when he spoke, and silence lingered between us.

Since he'd hidden the fact that he couldn't read from me as long as possible, I assumed he was ashamed.

"It's not your fault," I said softly. "I don't know the situation you grew up in, but you're smart. Once you have time to sit down and learn to read, I'm sure it'll come to you easily."

His eyes softened for a moment. But then he shrugged and did another survey of the bar, putting up his shield once again.

"I *want* to go upstairs and get Sage," I said, trying to

think of an excuse that wasn't the truth—that I was going to suggest a plan to Sage that Noah was totally going to hate. "When I was at the bar, that guy really creeped me out." I shuddered, since it was true—the fact that the demon had approached me and touched me *did* creep me out. "I just want to take a breather for a few minutes. If he tries anything while I'm up there, you can handle it, right?" I smiled and gave him my biggest doe eyes, hoping it would win him over and get him to cave.

I didn't like manipulating him like this. But there was no way he'd be okay with the plan I was formulating... and there was a chance that Sage might jump on board. So I had to tell her my idea. And I had to do it quickly, since none of us knew how long the demon would stay in this bar.

He nodded, seeming to accept my reasoning. "I'll walk you to the stairs," he finally said. "Come on."

"You don't think I can make it to the stairs by myself?" I rolled my eyes.

"You probably can," he said. "But remember your promise earlier?"

That I'd do as he said so he could keep me safe. How could I forget?

"All right," I agreed, since I needed to pick and choose my battles. "We'll be back down in a few minutes. If the target leaves, send a voice message. Okay?"

"Of course." He smirked, a determined glint flashing in his eyes. "After I've finished following him and vanquishing his ass."

RAVEN

*S*age was finishing up her walk around the upstairs area of the bar and was about to head back down when I found her.

"Raven?" she said when she saw me. "What're you doing up here? Noah told you to wait at the downstairs bar…"

"Noah found the demon," I said quickly. "Well, the demon found me."

"What do you mean?" Suspicion crossed over her gaze, and she looked around, clearly not wanting to be overheard.

Luckily, everyone else was either too drunk or too engrossed in conversation to be paying attention to what we were talking about. Because if anyone were listening in, it would have sounded pretty weird.

It still sounded weird to *me*, even though I knew about the supernatural world.

I pulled her to the bathroom—it was a single-holer, so we had privacy—and quickly updated her on everything that had happened downstairs. Well, I updated her on everything except for the way that Noah's kiss had made me feel like I was melting in his arms. My feelings toward him felt too private to share. Plus, this was a planning session—not a gossip session. There was a demon in this bar right now. We couldn't get distracted.

"Noah *kissed* you?" she said once I'd finished.

So much for not getting distracted.

"He wanted the demon to think I was taken and move onto another target." I shrugged, wanting to take the attention off that kiss. I wasn't sure when I'd be comfortable discussing it—if ever—but it certainly wasn't now. "That's why I came to talk to you—because this is the second demon who's found me in a bar and specifically targeted me."

Her phone pinged with a voice message. Noah. I nodded for her to take it, and she pressed play.

"The demon just headed upstairs," his recorded voice played back at us. "I have to stay down here to make sure he doesn't have a chance to leave. It's too public up there for the demon to try anything, but Sage, you better keep Raven safe." He sounded worried at the end there…

and kind of threatening, too. It was like he was warning Sage that she didn't want to find out what he'd do if she failed at keeping me out of the demon's clutches.

Sage and I looked at each other, understanding passing between us.

"So... there's something about you that the demons want." She lowered her voice—probably to make sure the demon couldn't hear us through the door.

"Bingo," I said, matching her hushed tone. "He's after me, just like Eli. Maybe it's also connected to why the demons are after my mom. I mean, we share the same DNA, so it would make sense that there's something about us that the demons want. Right?"

"The same *human* DNA," Sage said. "I've already told you—you and your mom don't smell different than any other humans. Plus, you drank the cloaking potion. Even if there *is* something about you that the demons are tracking, you should be off their radar now."

"Yet this is the second time I've been targeted." I placed my hands on my hips, unwilling to let her brush it off so easily. "He came right up to me at the bar. It can't be a coincidence."

She took a few seconds to think about it. "Noah's not going to like this," she finally said. "He's determined to keep you alive, and if the demons are targeting you, it puts you more at risk."

"It does." I spoke faster, excited now that I'd figured out a way to make myself useful. Or maybe I was just scared. The two emotions were blurring together so much that I couldn't tell them apart anymore. "But if I'm right that I'm being targeted—which I'm pretty sure I am—I was hoping we could use it to our advantage."

"How?" she asked.

"Easy." I smiled. "By using me as bait."

A few minutes later, we had a plan.

"Noah's *really* not going to like this," Sage said, although she smiled anyway—she was excited for what we were about to do. "But I think it'll work. So here it goes."

She took out her phone and replied to Noah's voice message with a voice message of her own. "Raven and I have a plan," she said once it started recording, continuing on to give him his exact instructions. It was crazy enough that it might work. Once done telling him what to expect, she sent the message and placed her phone back in her purse.

Then we linked arms and walked out of the bathroom.

The demon was standing directly across the way,

waiting his turn at the upstairs bar. But he was watching the bathroom door—clearly waiting for us.

He looked so unassuming in his preppy, frat guy clothing. It really was the perfect disguise for a demon on the prowl.

Internally, I shuddered with disgust. Externally, I plastered on a mega-watt smile and led Sage toward him.

If he was surprised we were approaching, he didn't show it.

"Hey again," I said once we reached him, tossing my hair over my shoulder in a way I hoped looked flirtatious. "Sorry about earlier. My ex can be a real jerk sometimes."

He stared at me—now that I knew what he was, I could tell that there was no trace of humanity in his gaze. "Ex?" he asked, tilting his head slightly to show he didn't fully believe me. "From that little display downstairs, it didn't look like he was your ex."

"It's complicated." I waved a hand in the air, hoping to make it clear that I didn't want to discuss it. "By the way, I'm Rose. This is my friend Sarah." I'd already learned during the long car ride from LA to New Orleans that while interacting with demons, we gave ourselves fake names to protect our real identities.

Those were the names we'd decided on for this hunt. Noah's fake name was Nick.

"Nice to meet you." He focused on me, barely paying Sage any attention. It was like she was invisible. "I'm Joe."

It took all of my effort not to laugh, since clearly, this demon's real name *wasn't* Joe.

"Hi, Joe," I said, twisting a strand of my hair around my finger. "I didn't mean to be so stingy at the bar. When I saw that my ex was here, I got sort of uptight. Ya know?" I sounded like a ditzy valley girl, but whatever. The more I could sell it, the better.

"I understand." He smiled and leaned closer, looking like I'd just dropped the world's best present into his lap. "But hey, this isn't the only bar in town. What do you think about checking out someplace else? Someplace where your ex *isn't* hanging around ready to pounce?"

I smiled right back at him. That had been easier than expected.

It also meant that this was really happening.

Nerves bundled inside my stomach. But I swallowed them down, forcing myself to stay calm.

"That sounds great," I said, somehow managing to sound excited as I motioned to the exit. "Please, lead the way."

RAVEN

I half expected Noah to come running up the stairs to stop Sage and I from going through with this, or to block us from exiting the bar.

Much to my relief, he went along with the plan—he was on the other side of the bar when we came down the stairs. He was pretending not to notice us, but I knew he was aware of our every move.

Once we left the bar, I also trusted that he wasn't far behind.

Joe stopped walking once we reached a side alley.

"Why'd you stop?" I asked.

"I know a cool place, but the fastest way to get there is through here," he said with a mischievous smile. "You girls game for an adventure?"

I had to stop myself from rolling my eyes. That

couldn't seriously work on people... could it? What girl would be dumb enough to walk into a dark, deserted alley with a guy she'd just met at a bar?

Judging by the way Joe seemed to think this was totally normal, I guessed the ploy had worked for him before.

There were some truly stupid people in this world.

And right now, I had to pretend to be one of them.

"I'm always game for an adventure." I matched his grin with one of my own.

There was going to be an adventure all right—just not the one he was planning on.

"Fantastic." He led the way into the alley, fiddling with his watch as he walked.

Sage and I gave each other knowing smirks behind his back and followed his lead.

"It's just this way..." He stopped again, pointing down a second alley branching off from the one we were in.

We just nodded—playing the part of innocent, trusting girls—and continued on. This alley was full of dumpsters and overflowing bins, and it smelled like rotting garbage. It reminded me of the alley behind the restaurant on the Pier that I'd been dragged into the night I was attacked.

Apparently, the demons had a system going on here.

Once we were halfway down the alley, the demon grabbed my wrist with his supernatural strength and held me in place. At the same time, he reached for a knife with his other hand and moved to slice Sage's neck.

Sage had her knife in hand faster than I could blink. She stopped Joe's knife before it could land a blow.

The demon's eyes went wide in surprise.

But he wasn't *so* surprised that he'd lost his grip on my wrist. And I couldn't break free with my pitiful human strength.

Sage made another move at him with her knife, but he blocked her attack.

At the same time, Noah rushed down the alley, his heavenly dagger in hand. I only knew it was a heavenly dagger because he'd told me so—and because it had nearly burned my hand when I'd tried to touch it. (Apparently, us mere humans couldn't hold heavenly weapons without being burned.) Otherwise, it looked no more magical than the knife Sage was using to attack.

Noah liked to call it a slicer—I guess he thought it sounded cooler than "heavenly dagger."

As the demon blocked another attack from Sage, Noah jumped on the opportunity to ram his slicer straight through the demon's heart.

The demon's mouth opened in horror, and for a

moment I saw his true form. Red eyes and elongated, yellow teeth that came down into sharp points.

But I didn't get to stare at his form for long, because he turned into a human-sized cloud of ash. The ash looked like it was floating in the air for a second. But it fell to a pile on the ground a moment later.

All that remained of Joe the demon were the sharp inhuman teeth on top of the pile of ash.

Noah reached down to collect a tooth, and I shook out my hand. The demon had been holding onto my wrist *tightly*.

Once Noah placed the tooth in his pocket and stood back up, he faced me, his eyes burning with anger. "What the hell were you thinking?" he said, his voice echoing through the alley. "Were you trying to get yourself killed?!"

I backed away, because right now, *he* was the one who looked like he wanted to kill *me*.

Before I could respond, someone materialized a few feet in front of us.

Azazel.

And judging from the greater demon's frown, the three of us were *not* who he was expecting to see.

"The trio from Santa Monica..." he said, apparently recognizing us from the ambush on the Pier. His gaze turned to me—I could have sworn he looked impressed

—and he asked, "How did you make your aura appear like—"

Noah didn't allow him to finish. He just reached for his weapons belt, grabbed his dart gun, and shot a dart straight into Azazel's neck while the demon was mid-sentence.

I had to hand it to him—Noah had kickass aim.

Azazel's hand went to the dart, and then he flashed out of the alley as suddenly as he'd appeared.

I knew exactly what potion had been inside that dart —it was the one Amber Devereux of the LA witch circle sold us before we left on our journey. It had the power to send anyone with teleportation powers back to the place they'd teleported from last, and to make them unable to teleport for the next few minutes.

It was the only weapon we had against Azazel, since only Nephilim could kill greater demons. So we had to make due with what we had.

"Why did you do that?" I motioned to the place where Azazel had just stood and turned to Noah, frustration blazing in my eyes. Now *I* was the angry one.

"Do what?" He placed the dart gun back into his belt. "Save all of our asses?"

"Cut him off mid-sentence," I said. "It sounded like he was going to tell us why the demons are after me. But you cut him off before he could finish!"

"We'll figure out what the demons want with you," Noah said. "Just not at the risk of your safety."

"I'm at risk while we're demon hunting no matter what." I held his gaze, refusing to back down. "I seriously can't believe you did that."

"I won't apologize for saving your life." Given his stern expression, I knew he meant it. He was one of the most stubborn people I'd ever met—beside myself, of course.

"Can we finish this conversation later?" Sage asked, looking back and forth between the two of us in irritation. "Because we need to get out of here. We only have five minutes until Azazel reappears."

She didn't have to say it twice.

Without another word, the three of us hurried back toward the hotel, wanting to put as much distance between us and that alley as possible.

*W*e didn't make it far before someone grabbed me out of nowhere and threw me into a brick wall.

I closed my eyes, bracing for impact.

Nothing happened.

When I opened my eyes, I was standing in a low-lit, dingy bar. A semi-circle of about twenty-five people surrounded me, all of them glaring at me as if I'd done something to seriously piss them off.

The person who had grabbed me—a woman in her thirties—was holding onto both of my wrists and had secured a handcuff around one of them. I glanced to the side and saw Noah, who was also being held down.

Sage wasn't far behind. She and another one of the

strong strangers materialized straight through the wall, like the bricks were made of nothing.

Both she and Noah were also cuffed.

"Rougarou," Sage muttered, glancing around at the people in the room. "Crap."

Noah tried to fight the person—the *rougarou*—restraining him. But two more of them—the two biggest guys in the room—quickly put a stop to that.

The three of us were hurled into three chairs around a table, our wrists cuffed to the legs of the table. Noah and Sage pulled as hard as they could against the cuff, but nothing happened.

"You can't escape." A woman a little younger than my mom stepped out from the center of the crowd, and everyone parted to let her through. She had long brown hair, startling gray eyes, and walked with the confidence of a warrior queen from ancient times. "The tables are bolted deep into the ground, and the cuffs are charmed with dark magic to resist even the strongest supernaturals and to prevent you from shifting."

That didn't stop Noah from mustering up all his strength and giving the cuff another tug.

Like the woman promised, nothing happened.

"What do you want from us?" Sage asked calmly, staring her down. "Are you working for the same people as the coyotes?"

The woman didn't reply. Instead, she approached us and pulled each of our cloaking rings off our fingers. She started with Sage, then moved onto Noah, then to me. Of course, when she got to me she didn't find a ring, since I was still depending on the potion. I wouldn't have my ring until tomorrow—if we were free from these rougarou by tomorrow.

"She's human," the woman who brought me through the wall spoke up. "She didn't have the strength of a supernatural."

The lady who had taken Noah and Sage's rings lifted her eyebrows in surprise. "A human?" she asked, staring at me with a mix of amazement and disdain. "What's a human doing traveling with two wolf shifters?"

Apparently, my current traveling situation could always be counted on to baffle supernaturals.

"Why did you drag us in here?" I answered her question with one of my own. "What do you want with us?"

Noah glared at me, clearly wanting me to shut up. But I couldn't help asking questions. We'd done nothing to these supernaturals. In fact, we'd *helped* them by vanquishing a demon that had been hunting in their city.

They should have been thanking us—not imprisoning us.

The woman placed the two cloaking rings on her fingers. Noah's was so large that it only fit around her thumb. Then she turned to face Sage. "You know exactly why you're here," she said with a knowing smile. "Don't you, Sage Montgomery?"

"The coyotes didn't tell me what they wanted with me," Sage replied with her chin held high. "So no—I don't know why we're here."

The woman narrowed her eyes at Sage. "Don't play me for a fool," she said. "The alpha of the rougarou pack deserves more respect than that."

So, this woman was the alpha. I wouldn't have guessed it—there were lots of men in the pack who looked physically stronger than she was—but I liked it. Girl power for the win.

She also had yet to attack. I hoped it was a sign that she might be willing to hear us out instead of trying to kill us like the coyotes had done.

"Montgomery pack members aren't allowed on our land," she continued. "We know what each and every member of your pack looks like. The moment we caught word that unknown wolf shifters were at the Voodoo Queen's store, I sent scouts to investigate. Imagine my surprise when I learned that Sage Montgomery herself was here." The tips of her fingers shifted into wolf form, so she could show off her deadly claws. "I should kill you on the spot."

"Don't," Sage said quickly. "We don't want any trouble. There was a demon in New Orleans, and my hunting partner and I came to vanquish him. We'd just finished before you found us and brought us here. We were heading back to our hotel, and were planning on leaving tomorrow. I swear it."

The alpha retracted her claws and stared down at Sage. For a moment I thought she was going to say okay and let us go... but there was no way it would be that easy.

"A demon?" She twisted the stolen cloaking rings around her fingers. "I heard rumors that demons escaped from a Hell Gate a few months ago, but I've yet to see one myself."

"It's not a rumor," Noah said. "It's true. We helped *all* the supernaturals of New Orleans by vanquishing the demon that was here. We don't want any trouble with your pack. Let us go, and we'll be out of here by midnight tomorrow."

"Why wait until tomorrow?" she asked. "*If* we let you live—and that's a serious if—you'll be expected to leave the moment you're released from our bar."

"Tomorrow by midnight," Sage bargained. "I'll make

a blood oath that we won't harm anyone in your pack for the duration of this visit."

I couldn't help noticing her wording—she specified that she wouldn't harm them *only* for the duration of this visit. Smart. If another time arose when we needed to fight against the rougarou, Sage wouldn't be bound by the oath she'd propositioned tonight, since it had a time limit.

"A blood oath with a Montgomery wolf." The alpha chuckled. "What a day this is turning into."

"So you'll do it?" Sage asked.

The alpha stood perfectly still and held Sage's gaze. Sage looked up at her for only a few seconds before lowering her eyes.

Time with the shifters allowed me to understand what was going on—Sage was showing submission to the rougarou alpha. I could tell by the way that Sage's jaw tensed that it pained her to submit so easily. But I understood why she was doing it. It was the best way to ensure our safety and to increase the chance of the rougarou setting us free.

"I'll consider it," the alpha replied. "Only after you tell me the truth about this so-called 'demon hunt' you're on."

Noah was quick to jump in. "The mission was given

to me by the Earth Angel Annika herself," he said. "She commanded me to—"

"Not yet." The alpha raised a hand to cut him off. From the way her gray eyes glimmered, I could tell she had a trick up her sleeve. "How am I supposed to believe any of you without you drinking a truth potion first?"

RAVEN

"**G**reat idea." Sage sat straighter, relief crossing her face. "I have some truth potion back at the hotel where we're staying. Let me get it, I'll bring it right back, and then I'll drink it and set this all straight."

The alpha burst into melodious laughter. "How gullible do you think I am?" she asked once she'd gotten control of herself. "First of all, we'll be using truth potion that *I've* purchased. Secondly, if I let you out of here, you'll run away and never look back."

"That's not true." Sage held her chin higher. "I'd never leave my friends behind."

"I'm not stupid enough to trust a Montgomery," she replied. "Especially one so eager to take truth potion.

Which leaves one of the two of you..." She glanced between Noah and me, as if deciding between us.

Noah focused on the wall straight ahead. His eyes were hard—I could tell he hated the mere thought of drinking truth potion. He was the most private person I knew. I had no idea what secrets he was keeping, but I knew that the last thing he wanted was to be forced to expose them in front of an entire pack of strangers.

I was going to have to be the one to drink the truth potion. Which was fine by me, since I wasn't hiding any big supernatural secrets from the rougarou. Once they heard the truth, I was positive that they'd let us go.

Problem was—if I volunteered, the alpha would likely choose Noah just to spite us all. And if I asked her *not* to pick me, she'd probably pick me just because I didn't want to be chosen.

Noah needed to volunteer. Because if he seemed eager to take the truth potion—like Sage had—the alpha would default to me. We'd reverse psychology the rougarou alpha without her realizing what we were doing.

Except I had no way of communicating the idea with Noah without the rougarou hearing my plan.

If my mom were in this situation, she'd tell me to will the universe to do what I wanted. She'd tell me to think about what I wanted and *manifest* it into happening. Because she literally believed that people could manifest "gifts" from the universe into coming true if they wanted it badly enough.

I'd always thought it was crazy-talk. But right now, I had nothing to lose.

So I took a deep breath, preparing myself. The first thing my mom would tell me to do was to get rid of my doubt that manifesting could work. Apparently, if I doubted manifestation worked, I was *asking* the universe to prove it didn't work. So I needed to trust in it myself. I needed to let go of my disbelief.

The idea of manifestation had always seemed so ridiculous to me that I wasn't sure I could let go of my doubt.

Then again, I used to think that witches, shifters, spells, potions, demons, angels, and everything else in the supernatural world didn't exist, either.

Why should manifesting be any different?

The rougarou alpha was studying Noah and me, like she was close to making a decision. I needed to hurry up and manifest my will into happening.

Volunteer, I thought, staring straight at Noah and trying to will him—and the universe—to listen to my pleas. *If you volunteer, she'll choose me. I know you don't want to be forced to spill your secrets in front of all these people. So volunteer. Be eager about it like Sage was. Volun-*

teer, volunteer, volunteer... I repeated it, trying to *will* Noah to know what I desired.

It felt silly, and I was beginning to think I was being delusional in thinking this could work.

Until Noah straightened, looked the alpha straight in the eye, and laughed. "Why do you even need to think about this?" he asked. "You're seriously having trouble choosing between me—a shifter—and a *human?*" He spoke the name of my race like humans were worthless and puffed out his chest in pride. "This is *my* demon hunt. I'll take the truth potion, we can get all of this straightened out, and you can send us on our way. It'll be easy. Just choose me."

"Thank you for making my decision for me." The alpha was calm as she spoke, and she zeroed in on me. "The one who will be taking the truth potion is the human."

*T*he alpha sent one of her minions to fetch the truth potion from behind the bar. Apparently, they kept a stock of different potions back there.

I tried to meet Noah's gaze so I could let him know he'd done the right thing, but he was refusing to look at me.

Maybe I'd read him wrong? Maybe he really *had* wanted to take the truth potion?

Honestly, that was more likely than him having volunteered because I'd somehow "manifested" him into understanding my plan.

"You've got this," Sage said to me, and I focused on her, glad to find her looking at me like she believed in me. "Just tell the truth. Not like you'll have an option.

But really—the truth will set us free. Literally, in this case."

I didn't know how she had it in her to joke at a time like this, but I smiled, grateful for the encouragement.

A tall rougarou man returned with a vial of light blue potion and handed it to the alpha. I still didn't know the alpha's name, but I doubted formal introductions were going to happen until she decided she could trust us or not.

She pulled a chair up right in front of me and situated herself in it. "What do you know about truth potion, human?" she asked.

"My name is Raven." I didn't care what prejudices the supernaturals had against humans—I was a person, and I deserved to be called by my name. "And I know that after someone drinks truth potion, they'll be magically bound to tell the truth as they know it."

The last bit was the most important part—the truth potion could only get people to tell the truth *as they knew it*. If I didn't know the answer to a question, I wouldn't be able to answer it truthfully, no matter how strong the potion was. Also, if what I believed to be the truth was actually incorrect, I'd still answer with the truth as I believed it to be.

"Very good, Raven," the alpha said. She wasn't being warm and fuzzy, but at least she was acknowledging my name. "Either your companions taught you well, or you knew about the supernatural world before meeting them. I suppose we'll find out soon, won't we?"

I didn't have time to reply before she uncapped the vial, reached forward, and emptied the light blue liquid down my throat.

RAVEN

The truth potion tasted fruity and sweet, like the light blue shaved ice I used to love eating at fairs.

A few seconds later, I felt calm and relaxed. On one level, I knew this was because I'd just consumed truth potion. But the rougarou around me no longer looked threatening. All of the tension I'd felt since being pulled through the brick wall and into their supernatural bar disappeared.

I still didn't like that I was handcuffed to a chair, but I understood why they'd done it. They didn't want to risk us attacking them.

Noah and Sage were strong shifters—the rougarou were right to be afraid.

But once they knew the truth about why we were

here, they'd unlock the handcuffs and let us go. Maybe they'd even support our hunt. After all, the demons were our common enemy. We should be teaming up—not abducting each other from the street and handcuffing each other to tables.

My head and body felt fuzzy, like I was an onlooker to our current situation instead of a part of it. But I'd do what needed to be done and tell the rougarou everything I knew.

I wouldn't let Noah and Sage down.

"The potion has taken hold," the alpha said. Her voice was warm and sweet, like a nurturing mother. I must have imagined the harshness from before. "Now, Raven, please tell me. How did you end up traveling with these two shifters chained beside you?"

I told her the exact same, *true* story that I'd told the Voodoo Queen at her shop, starting from the night of my twenty-first birthday. The alpha occasionally asked additional questions to push me to continue, and I answered truthfully without fail. Eventually, I ended up where we were right now, with the three of us handcuffed in the middle of her bar.

"What is your relationship with both Sage and Noah?" she asked. It hadn't taken her long to learn Noah's name, since he was integral in my story. According to her, it was a pretty common name amongst wolves. Like the wolf equivalent to the human name John.

"Sage and I are friends," I said, since that answer was easy. "Noah and I..." I stopped, suddenly stuck on how to answer. What *were* Noah and I?

I couldn't answer with the truth because I didn't know the answer. In fact, I'd wanted to ask Noah the same question all night. Because after that kiss, I had no idea where the two of us stood.

My cheeks heated, and I couldn't bring myself to look at him. How was I supposed to be honest about my feelings for him when I wasn't sure *what* those feelings were myself?

I couldn't. So I'd have to settle with the bare facts.

"Noah took me on this mission because Rosella recommended he do so, and he seemed to trust Rosella," I said. "Our relationship is complicated. We don't get along most of the time, but when it comes down to it, I know he's doing everything he can to keep me safe. I trust him with my life."

It was the truth, and I meant every word of it.

"Interesting." The alpha didn't let a single reaction slip through her expression. "So the three of you didn't come here with an intent to harm the rougarou?"

"We never wanted to harm you," I said. "We *don't* want to harm you. All we wanted to do was slay the demon. Now we just need to finish up our business with the Voodoo Queen tomorrow evening, and get out of here."

"What more business do you have with the Voodoo Queen?" she asked.

"Tomorrow evening we're picking up a cloaking ring she's making for me." The words tumbled out of my mouth before I could contemplate if the rougarou alpha should know the exact details of our appointment. "Then she'll do a tracking spell to find another demon for us to hunt, and we'll head off to whatever city she sends us to."

She said nothing for a few seconds, and I wondered if she was done.

"Your story is fascinating, Raven," she finally said. "Given the fact that you're a human, you're handling all of this very well. So I do have one more question for you."

"All right," I said, ready for anything.

"Prior to your initial run-in with Noah and Sage, did you have any other encounters with the supernatural world?"

I opened my mouth to say no.

But I couldn't say it.

Because I wasn't sure if that was the truth or not.

"I don't know," I said honestly.

"You don't know?" the alpha repeated, tilting her head in curiosity. "How can that be? The answer should be straightforward. Either yes or no."

I didn't know because I hadn't been honest—*totally* honest—with anyone about what had happened to me this past winter.

According to everyone I knew, I'd made a spur of the moment decision to go backpacking in Europe, didn't tell anyone I was leaving, and stayed there for weeks. I remembered doing that—sort of. But the memories were hazy.

So hazy that I questioned whether or not they'd happened at all.

It had come up in conversation with Noah once, briefly. When it did, I'd done what I always did when Europe came up and changed the subject. Mainly because I didn't want him to think I was crazy.

But it was time to admit what I'd been wondering since learning about the supernatural world and finding out that my mom and I were somehow connected to it. That maybe there was something more going on with my spur of the moment vacation and hazy memories of it than I realized.

"Over the winter, I took a trip to Europe for a few weeks," I said slowly, swallowing as I prepared to continue. I wasn't sure why I was telling the alpha this—

I didn't think it was relevant to helping her realize that Noah, Sage, and I weren't here to hurt the rougarou.

But I also had a feeling that if I told her the truth, she could help me. And I needed help more than ever.

"Disappearing like that without telling anyone wasn't like me," I continued. "And the memories of the trip are so hazy that it's like I wasn't there at all. So I can't help wondering if there might be something more going on with what happened. Something *supernatural.*"

She leaned forward, looking more curious than ever. "When you think about your trip, does it feel like you're watching someone else's experiences and not your own?" she asked. "Like the memories aren't quite *real?* Like you keep hitting a wall, but that if you pushed at the wall hard enough, it would dissolve and re-form into something else entirely?"

"Exactly." I perked up, amazed that she knew what I was going through. "How did you know that?"

"Because you're right that there's something super-natural going on." She watched me closely, her mouth set in a grim line. "Someone has tampered with your memories."

"*W*hat do you mean?" I sat back in shock. "How could my memories have been tampered with?"

It sounded so strange to say... but it didn't sound *wrong* either.

It certainly made more sense than the possibility that I'd run off to Europe on a whim, or that I was having some kind of psychotic delusion.

"My guess would be that you never went to Europe at all," she said simply. "And that someone—a supernatural of some sort—used a memory potion to alter your memories."

"But that's impossible," I said. "Sage taught me about memory potions. They can only alter memories that go back a few days, tops. I was in Europe for *weeks*. Not even a memory potion could change my memories that much."

"It's true that the memory potions available on the market will only be able to alter a few days worth of memories," she said. "But the witches who sell their magic are far from the strongest witches in the world. Even the strongest witches—like the ones in the Voodoo Queen's circle and the Devereux LA circle—aren't nearly as strong as the witches employed by the five vampire kingdoms."

I nodded, since I'd learned about those five kingdoms during the long drive with Noah and Sage. "A small number of witches live in the vampire kingdoms, and those witches perform magic for the vampires in exchange for an extravagant lifestyle," I shared the bit I knew about those witches.

"Precisely." She nodded. "The witches living in the vampire kingdoms are the strongest witches in the world. Not many of them have the power to erase a few *weeks* worth of memories—but there are certainly a few who could."

I sat back, the revelation strangely comforting since it explained so much of what had been eating away at me recently. A witch had altered my memories. I wasn't sure why a witch would want to do that, but now that I was aware my memories had been erased, there had to be a way to fix this.

"So how do I get my memories back?" I asked.

Because there had to be a way to get them back. Right?

"You'd have to find the witch who took them away in the first place," she said. "Only that witch can give you a reversal pill that will return your memories to you."

"Great." I huffed. "How am I supposed to find this witch when she—or he—took away the memories I have of who they are?"

"The witch is most likely a she," the alpha said.

"All the witches I've met so far are female," I realized. "Why? Do male witches not exist at all?"

"They exist," Sage cut in. "But female witches have more powerful magic than their male counterparts. No one knows why—it's just the way witch magic works. They joke that magic must be carried on the X chromosome, so men only get half the amount of magic as women."

"Oh," I said. "Interesting."

"Anyway, back to your question about how to find the witch who erased your memories," the alpha said. "I agree that it's a difficult predicament. I don't have an answer for you, but the Earth Angel has connections throughout the supernatural world. If there's anyone who might be able to help you, it's her."

"Yet another reason why I need to get to Avalon," I said.

Which meant if I wanted any chance of keeping my sanity, I'd have to shelf my curiosity about my erased memories for now. Just like how I was trying to shelf my worry about my mom. It was tough, because I had so many questions, but completing the demon hunt and getting to Avalon needed my full attention. With my mom's life on the line, I couldn't afford to get distracted.

"But while I don't have an answer for you, someone else here might." The alpha turned to Noah, glaring at him. "We know little about Noah, or where he comes from. Perhaps he had something to do with your memories being erased?"

"Wait." I held up a hand, stopping her. "Noah didn't erase my memories. He had nothing to do with this."

"So trusting," the alpha said to me. "You have much to learn, little human."

There she went again, calling me *human* instead of using my name. I really hated that.

"Raven's right," Noah spoke up. "If her memories were erased, I had nothing to do with it. I swear it. I'll even take a truth potion to prove it."

"Truth potion doesn't come cheap," the alpha said. "There's a reason why we only used one vial for the three of you. For now, you and Sage will remain detained until I figure out how to proceed."

My stomach swirled with worry about what might happen to Noah and Sage. "Don't hurt them," I begged. "Please. They're on my side."

"Or so you think." She pressed her lips together, looking unconvinced.

"Maybe someone gave me a memory potion, but if Noah says it's not him, I believe him," I said. "He wouldn't lie. Not about this."

"Give him the truth potion," Sage cut in. "I'll pay you double what the potion cost you. You'll have nothing to lose."

"It's not a bad offer," she said, looking Sage over. "I'll consider it. But first, I'd like to continue my conversation with Raven here." She said my name with more respect than earlier, turning her focus back to me.

"I told you everything I know," I said.

"I know you did," she said. "But you should know that for most people—including supernaturals— memory potions go undetected. The person who took the memory potion can't tell a difference between the implanted memories and reality. It wouldn't feel hazy, like you described. It would simply feel real."

"But I can tell the difference between the fake memories and the real ones," I said. "Why?"

"Sometimes, if a supernatural is stronger than the witch who brewed the potion, they'll be able to resist the potion," she said. "But you're not a supernatural. There's no doubt that you're a human—and a delicious-smelling human, at that."

I wasn't sure whether to take that as a compliment or be afraid that she might want to taste me.

I settled with asking her another question.

"So you have no idea why I can tell that my memories have been tampered with?" I asked.

"There are occasional humans who are able to resist magic," she said. "Psychics. But these humans are rare— I've never met one myself—and they always have a unique ability of their own."

I perked up at the word "ability." My mom had always said she had a special *ability* to read tarot cards, and she'd insisted that I had an ability of my own. I never thought I did, but she was convinced I'd realize what it was sooner or later.

"My mom has the ability to read tarot cards." I was aware that the truth potion was making me comfortable enough to say all of this to the alpha, but at the same time, I didn't care. If being honest helped me understand what was happening to me, then so be it. Let the truth set me free. "She always calls herself a witch, but psychic would describe her pretty well, too."

"And you?" She leaned forward, looking like she was onto something. "Have you inherited her gift?"

"I don't have an ability." I shrugged. "I'm definitely *not* a psychic."

If I were, maybe that would explain why demons were after me. But nope. I didn't have any special abilities. I'd know if I did.

"Hmm." She watched me carefully, looking intrigued and not convinced. But I was under the truth potion, so she had no choice but to believe me.

It was a relief to be able to be honest and know that the person I was talking to wouldn't doubt me. Not that I would want to take truth potion all the time—there were plenty of instances where it was good to hide the truth—but there was something freeing about knowing that I was being believed one hundred percent.

"Since I can tell when my memories have been tampered with, I promise I haven't been given any memory potion since Noah and Sage saved me from that demon in Santa Monica," I told her. "They haven't messed with my memories. I'd know if they had."

"They haven't messed with your memories since you met them at the Pier," she said. "That doesn't mean they weren't involved in whatever happened to you this winter."

"So take up Sage's offer," Noah cut in. "Give me truth

potion, and *then* ask me if I was involved with Raven's memories being erased. Because I promise my answer will stay the same."

"*I* think I'll do that," she said. "Jack, go get another vial of truth potion and bring it to me."

The same rougarou who'd gotten my truth potion—Jack—went behind the bar and brought out another light blue vial. I was amazed by how easily the alpha had agreed to the idea, but relieved nonetheless. I was sure Sage's offer to pay her double what the potion was worth had a big part to do with her agreement.

People always seemed to become *much* more agreeable when money was involved. Specifically, when they would be getting a large amount of it.

Jack handed the alpha the potion. Then, just like she did for me, the uncapped the vial and brought it to Noah's lips so he could drink.

I didn't like her touching him—a strange sort of protectiveness came over me, like Noah was *mine* and no one else should be touching him, especially another woman—but I swallowed down the urge to tell her to back off. This was no time for my crush on him to get in the way of anything.

A few seconds after swallowing the potion, his eyes dilated. It must have started working.

I prayed that the alpha would only ask him if he'd given me the memory potion, and nothing more. I didn't know what Noah was hiding about his past, but I had a feeling that whatever it was, he didn't want the rougarou to know.

The alpha scooted her chair so she was directly in front of him and placed her hands on her thighs, looking ready for an interrogation. "Noah," she said, her voice calm and relaxed. "Have you ever given Raven a memory potion?"

"I haven't," he answered, concise as always.

"Do you know who gave her the memory potion that erased whatever happened to her while she thinks she was in Europe?"

"No."

"All right." The alpha looked convinced. "I believe that you know nothing about Raven's memory wipe— that whatever happened to her was caused by supernaturals before you met. However, I don't believe in coincidences, so you must have met for a reason."

Noah didn't reply to that. He just watched the alpha closely. His fingers were tense—I could tell that all he wanted was to be freed from the handcuffs so we could all get out of there.

"Great," Sage said with a forced smile. "Now that we've worked everything out, will you agree to a truce until we leave tomorrow night?"

"Patience," the alpha said, still focused on Noah. "Since you're under the truth potion, I do have a few more questions for you."

The worry that had twisted my stomach before intensified.

Noah simply watched her, waiting.

"Your cause to get to Avalon is a noble one." She turned away from Noah to face her pack, and I relaxed slightly, getting the feeling that she was on our side now. "The Earth Angel needs as many fighters as possible to join her army in the war against the demons. We all need to band together to overcome this terrible threat. Therefore, I will not blame any rougarou who choose to leave the pack in favor of joining Annika's army."

Surprised chatter broke out amongst the rougarou at this announcement.

They only quieted once the alpha raised a hand to silence them.

"But in order for the rougarou to have the option to join the Earth Angel's army, they need to know where to go to do so," she continued, turning back to Noah. "Therefore, I need to know—where is the island of Avalon located?"

I felt Noah's relief at her line of questioning as if it were my own. I wasn't sure how that was possible, but I just *knew* she wasn't asking him anything he wasn't comfortable answering.

"I don't know," he said, looking straight at her as he spoke. "The location of Avalon is top secret—only Annika and her inner circle know where it is on a map."

"But you're leading Sage and Raven to Avalon once you collect the remaining three demon teeth," the alpha said. "Surely you know how to get there?"

"There is a liaison point," he said. "The vampire kingdom of the Vale in the Rocky Mountains of Canada. Go there, and tell King Alexander that you want to join the Earth Angel's army. All potential recruits will be assessed to determine if they're allowed entry or not. If allowed, they will be brought to Avalon."

"And if denied?" she asked.

"I'm just another potential soldier." He sounded more modest than I'd ever heard him sound before. "I don't know the details of how the process works. But my guess is that those who are denied are sent back home."

"Interesting," she said, and then she turned to address her pack again. "Let it be known that if any rougarou are denied entrance to Avalon, they will be welcomed back into the pack with open arms. I do not want fear of abandonment to hold you back from supporting a worthy cause. We are a family, and as your alpha, I will support your decisions no matter what. Understood?"

"Understood," they repeated in unison.

She nodded to them and turned back to us. "I'm afraid I haven't had a chance yet to properly introduce myself," she said. "I'm Leia, and as you know, I'm the alpha of the rougarou pack."

"Nice to meet you," I said, since it was nice to finally have a name to put to her face.

"I'm sorry the circumstances had to be what they were, but it's always better to be careful than be killed," she said. "Now—Sage Montgomery." She zeroed in on Sage. "What is the Montgomery pack doing to prepare to fight the demons?"

I was surprised she was addressing Sage, since Sage was the only one of the three of us who hadn't taken truth potion. But I supposed Leia knew that neither Noah nor I knew the details of what the Montgomery pack was doing. She also must have fully trusted us now.

Either that or she didn't want to use up any more precious truth potion.

I suspected it was the latter.

"I'm not sure," Sage answered. "We have a stronghold at our compound in LA, and Flint told me he's working on a plan. In the meantime, my focus is on helping Noah. He belongs in Avalon, and I want to help him get there."

"Why do you care so much about his cause?" Leia asked. "I haven't picked up any signs of a mate bond between the two of you. Have you imprinted on one another?"

"No," Sage and Noah said at the same time, both of them backing up like the idea of being imprinted on each other horrified them.

They looked at each other and chuckled, amused that they'd had such similar reactions.

"Noah's like a brother to me," Sage continued. "I'm helping him because he's a good person, and he deserves my help. Also, I enjoy the thrill of the hunt. It's a *lot* more interesting than sitting around the LA compound waiting for Flint to decide what to do against the demons."

"Has Flint given the Montgomery pack the same permission that I gave the rougarou?" she asked. "Permission to offer themselves to the Earth Angel's army, but still be allowed to return to the pack if refused?"

"No." Sage's eyes darkened. "Flint is a believer in the old ways. He also believes that the Montgomery wolves will be most useful against the demons from our compound—not from Avalon. Anyone who leaves the pack for Avalon will not be welcomed back."

"Yet here you are, away from your pack and helping Noah on his quest."

"What can I say?" Sage shrugged, giving Leia a small smile. "I get special privileges for being his favorite sister."

"You're his *only* sister," Noah cut in.

Sage flashed him a grin. "Which naturally makes me his favorite."

From the way the two of them acted around each other, it seemed more like *Noah* was Sage's brother—not big, scary Flint.

"I respect your independence," Leia decided. "Especially because you've used that independence to help a friend instead of hiding inside the Montgomery compound. The rougarou may not be aligned with the Montgomery pack—and this doesn't change that—but we are allied with *you* Sage Montgomery. And Noah and Raven, of course."

"Thank you," I said, relieved by her decision.

"You're welcome," she said. "The three of you have my permission to remain in New Orleans for as long as you wish. The punishment for any rougarou who tries to hurt you will be death. This will hold after you leave New Orleans, unless our alliance is broken. I'll send word to the rest of the rougarou once you leave."

She removed a key from her pocket and unlocked our handcuffs. Once freed, I flexed my fingers a few times, rubbing the place on my wrists where the metal had cut into my skin.

The air was still tense between the rest of the rougarou and the three of us, but it was a massive relief to know they weren't going to attack again.

"So," I said with a smile, hoping to lighten up the situation. "How long until this truth potion wears off?"

"I'll give you the antidote pills as a token of my good-will," Leia decided. "I'll also give you back these." She removed the cloaking rings from her fingers and handed them back to Noah and Sage. "You'll likely be relieved to know that there's a cloaking spell around this bar, so whoever you're hiding from wouldn't have been able to track you while your rings were off."

That *was* a huge relief, seeing as they'd snatched us while we'd been making a run from Azazel.

Her lackey—which was how I was thinking of Jack, the big rougarou who kept retrieving the truth potion for us—went behind the bar again. He returned with two antidote pills and handed them to us.

I took mine immediately, chewing the chalky pink tablet and swallowing it down. Noah did the same. I wasn't sure if the relief I felt once the tablets were in our systems was his or mine. I think it was a mix of both.

"I'm glad we had this talk tonight," Leia said as she walked us to the door. "I'm happy we came to an understanding before any drastic measures were taken. And I truly wish you the best of luck in your quest for Avalon."

With that, she sent us on our way, not allowing us to ask her or the rest of the rougarou pack any more questions.

RAVEN

The three of us didn't speak as we hurried from the supernatural bar back to the hotel. I think we just wanted to get back as quickly as possible, lest some other unknown supernatural threat emerge and threaten our lives tonight.

Luckily there were no signs of Azazel, and we made it back safely.

The moment we shut the door to our suite, Noah turned to me with fire blazing in his eyes. "Now you can finally answer my question," he said with so much anger that it seemed like he was about to explode then and there.

I stepped back in surprise. It seemed like forever since the rougarou had snatched us, but I knew exactly what question he was referring to. The memory of it flashed through my mind—the question he'd asked after we'd slain Joe the demon.

He wanted to know what I was thinking by walking off with Joe instead of letting him handle the situation his way.

"The demons clearly want me for a reason, and they're able to sniff me out of a crowd—even *after* I drank the cloaking potion." I held his gaze, not willing to show any doubt regarding my plan. If I did, he'd reject it in a heartbeat. Well, he'd likely reject my plan in a heartbeat no matter what, but if I were confident about it, maybe he'd give it some consideration later. "We should use this knowledge to our advantage and use me as bait."

Noah blinked a few times and stared at me, as if what I'd said was absurd. "Absolutely not," he said, the decision sounding final.

"Why not?" I asked. "It worked tonight."

"Because it puts you at more risk than necessary," he said. "Sage and I hunted demons just fine without you. We didn't need bait before, so we certainly don't need you to act as bait now."

We all remained standing in the center of the living room, way too worked up from everything that had just happened to sit down. At some point while Noah and I were talking, Sage must have turned on the electronic fireplace. As it crackled and burned, it reflected the tension sizzling in the air between us.

"I know that you were fine hunting demons without me," I said. "You've only reminded me a gazillion times. But compared to the other times you've hunted demons, did this hunt go faster or slower?"

"There was no difference," Noah said.

At the same time Sage said, "Faster. Definitely faster."

I turned to Sage, trusting her more than Noah in this instance. "Do you think using me as bait made the hunt tonight go faster?" I asked. "Or was it just a coincidence?"

She looked at Noah, guilt crossing her features. I sort of got it—they were hunting partners. She met him before she met me, so her loyalty was to him. She didn't want to say anything that might upset him.

But a faster hunt meant I could get to Avalon sooner, and therefore save my mom sooner. I didn't like upsetting Noah, but my mom's life came first. My desperation to save her was so strong that I could practically feel it coming off my body in waves. If acting as bait helped the hunt, I needed them to let me keep doing it. I needed them to help me save my mom.

"It was faster because of you," Noah admitted, running his hand through his hair as if he couldn't believe he was giving in.

I stilled, shocked that he'd given in, too. I'd expected a big, blow up fight—not for him to say I was right. It was almost like I'd manifested my desires onto him—again.

Maybe this manifesting thing wasn't as crazy as I'd always thought.

"How much faster?" I asked.

Immediately afterward, I thought, *Please, answer honestly.* I tried to manifest my desire for him to answer honestly, because hey, why not? Manifesting seemed to be on my side so far. I might as well go with what worked.

"We always have to wait for the demon to leave a public area—this can take anywhere from thirty minutes to hours," he said. "A few times, we've lost demons while they were in the crowd. Then we had to go back to the witch in that city to do another tracking spell to find the demon again. That can put us back by a day, sometimes more. Three times, we lost the demon completely."

"So we *have* to use me as bait," I said. "That way, we'll never lose the demons. They'll come right to us. Well, to me. All we have to do is let the demons lure us away, like we did tonight. They'll think they have the upper hand. Then we'll catch them off guard and attack."

"The demon tonight lured us straight to the liaison

spot he had with Azazel," Noah said. "If we didn't have that potion Amber made us, we would have been toast."

His words echoed in the air, and the three of us didn't say a word. Because Noah was right. Since none of us were Nephilim, none of us could kill Azazel.

We needed to avoid running into the greater demon again.

"How does teleporting work?" I asked. "Can Azazel teleport anywhere he wants?"

If he could, that was going to make this extra tricky.

"All I know about teleporting is how the witches do it," Sage said. "But it should be the same thing. They can only teleport someplace they've seen before. Which means they need to have been there before, or at least seen a picture."

"Perfect," I said. "So the demons clearly have 'drop off' spots where Azazel knows to expect them with the human they've collected. Places Azazel has seen, since he teleports in."

"That makes sense." Sage nodded. "But how did Azazel know to be there at the right time?"

"I don't know." I paused, thinking back to everything that had happened before the attack. "Joe fiddled with his smart watch before we went inside the second alley. Maybe he sent Azazel a message?"

"I noticed that too," she said. "That could be it. Did

you notice Eli on his phone or watch before he pulled you into the alley in Santa Monica?"

"I was in the bathroom before he pulled me into the alley," I said. "So no, I didn't. But he definitely had a phone on him. I saw him looking at it at the bar."

Sage pressed her lips together, as if thinking it over. "It's hard to picture demons using cell phones," she finally said. "But we use them on our hunts, so it's possible. And I don't have any other ideas." She shrugged and turned to Noah. "What do you think?" she asked him.

"I guess it's possible," he said. "Especially since as far as I'm aware, demons aren't telepathic."

"This actually works perfectly with my plan," I said. "Since the demons have arranged meeting spots with Azazel, we'll bring them to a private place to fight on *our* terms—not on theirs."

"And once Azazel realizes his demon scout is missing, it'll be too late for him to track the scout, because the scout will be dead." Sage gave me a high five, and for the first time, it truly felt like we were a team. "I love this plan. It's going to make our hunts *so* much more efficient."

"Thanks." I smiled, thrilled to have finally contributed and have it be appreciated. Then I turned back to Noah, hoping he agreed. "What do you think?"

"I don't like putting you straight into the line of fire,"

he said. "But you need to get to Avalon as quickly as possible, and I can't deny that this plan will make our hunt go faster. So I'll agree... as long as *you* agree to learn basic defense skills."

"Really?" I asked, shocked.

"Do I strike you as the type to say things I don't mean?" he asked.

"No," I said. "But a few days ago, you said I didn't have time to learn self defense skills because we had to focus on the hunt."

"A few days ago, I figured you would stay back where the demons couldn't see you while Sage and I did the hunting," he said. "Plus, the Voodoo Queen only gets to her store after sunset. Which means we'll have all day tomorrow to start basic training—and an entire private patio at our disposal to train on. If you're up for it, of course."

I glanced at the massive patio attached to our room, which looked out over the glowing New Orleans skyline. It was the perfect place for training. It would be just like those montage scenes I loved in movies.

"Of course I'm up for it," I said. "Consider me your new Padawan."

"My new what?" He tilted his head, confused.

Right—Noah was beyond behind on pop culture. I

should have realized he would miss the Star Wars reference.

"Teach me everything you know," I said instead.

"We'll start with the basics." He smiled for what felt like the first time since we'd gotten to New Orleans. "The skills you'll need to stay alive until Sage or I can take over in a fight. Not that it'll take me long to jump in—but it's better to be safe than sorry."

"You mean it's better to be safe than dead," I said.

He winced when I said the word *dead*, like the thought of anything happening to me pained him. "That's not going to happen," he promised. "You might be making it more difficult by volunteering as bait, but you're going to survive this hunt and get to Avalon. I'm seeing to that myself."

The whole time we'd been talking, we'd both been inching closer and closer toward each other. Now he stood straight in front of me, so close we were nearly touching.

My eyes instinctively went to his lips, and I thought back to when he'd kissed me. So much had happened since then with the rougarou, but that kiss felt as fresh as ever.

I wanted him to kiss me again.

From the way he was staring down at me, with heat

blazing in his eyes, I had a feeling he was thinking the exact same thing.

"All right then." Sage cleared her throat, reminding us that she was still there. "I'm glad that's all settled."

I stepped back from Noah, my cheeks flushing in embarrassment. What had come over me? It was like he'd cast some kind of spell over me. Or made me drink a love potion.

Except that from what Sage had taught me about potions, love potions didn't exist. There were rare, complicated potions to make people fall *out* of love, but it was impossible to make anyone fall *in* love.

Not that I was in love with Noah. I just met him. Plus, we could never be together because of the whole wolf imprinting and mating thing.

This was a crush. That was all.

Maybe if I kept telling myself that, I'd eventually believe it.

"I guess we should get ready for bed," I said, forcing myself to stop thinking about whatever my feelings were for Noah. "Since we have a long day ahead tomorrow, with me learning how to fight and all."

"No!" Sage said suddenly. "I mean, first I need to shower." She pointed to the bedroom door and started walking toward it, her eyes dancing in amusement.

"Didn't you just shower a few hours ago?" I asked.

"Yeah," she said. "But now I stink of rougarou." She made a big show of taking a deep breath, smelling herself, and crinkling her nose in disgust. "I'm *not* going to bed without showering first."

I glared at her, since what she was doing was obvious.

She hadn't forgotten that I'd told her about Noah kissing me to make Joe the demon back off, and she was making an excuse to give us space to talk alone.

I hated her and loved her for it at the same time.

Because the easiest thing to do was to pretend the kiss didn't happen. I could push my feelings for Noah aside, and we could continue on exactly as we'd been— barely tolerating each other and eager to get to Avalon so we could go our separate ways.

That would be the smart thing to do, since I'd never be the one for him. It was what I *should* do.

But that was easier said than done… especially now that Sage had disappeared into the bathroom faster than I could blink, leaving Noah and me alone.

"So..." I looked everywhere but at Noah, unsure where to start.

"So." Was that... amusement I heard in his tone? It couldn't be.

But when I forced myself to get a grip and look at him, he most definitely looked amused.

"What?" I asked.

He tilted his head in confusion. *Mock* confusion. "I didn't say anything," he said.

I paced around the room, wishing Sage hadn't left us alone.

Because this was worse than I'd thought it would be. He was acting like the kiss hadn't happened at all.

Wasn't that exactly what I'd hoped he would do only seconds earlier?

Except it wasn't what I *really* hoped he would do. Because I couldn't pretend that kiss hadn't happened. If I tried, I was just going to replay it over and over again in my mind, wondering if he'd been affected like I had.

If we didn't talk about it, I wasn't going to be able to focus on the most important thing I needed to concentrate on right now—training to make sure I didn't get killed. Which meant we had to talk about it. I could literally *die* if we didn't.

And since he clearly wasn't going to bring it up, I supposed it was on me.

"So… what was that about at the bar?" I asked, figuring it was best to just be out with it.

"What was what about at the bar?" He walked over to the big armchair and stretched out on it, clearly enjoying this.

Ugh. He was going to make me say it out loud.

I stayed standing, too wound up to sit. "You kissed me," I said, looking at him straight on. "Why?"

"That demon had his eye on you," he said simply. "I didn't like the way he was looking at you and touching you. He needed to know that you weren't his for the taking."

I raised an eyebrow. "And kissing me was the best way to do that?"

"What are you getting at?" His eyes were playful, and I couldn't help feeling like he was toying with me. Again.

Hadn't I already told him *not* to toy with me?

"What I'm *getting at* is that you didn't have to kiss me to get the demon to back off." I threw my hands down to my sides, annoyed that he was being so dense about this. "There had to have been other ways to do it."

"Maybe." He shrugged. "But my way worked."

How was he remaining so calm, when just *thinking* about the kiss made me turn into a bumbling idiot?

"That's not the point." I tried to get a grip on myself, but it was impossible when he was looking at me with so much fire in his eyes—like he wanted to kiss me again.

Why was it that whenever he looked at me like that, I was knocked completely speechless?

"So enlighten me, Raven," he said, still sounding as amused as ever. "What *is* your point?"

"My point is that you can't just go around kissing me like that." I crossed my arms, determined to stand my ground. "It's not fair."

"Fair?" He raised an eyebrow. "I was doing my job—keeping you safe from a demon. We all have parts to play in this hunt, Raven. Mine is to keep you safe. And to vanquish the demons, of course." He flipped his hair away from his eyes, as if killing demons was the most natural thing in the world to him. "You're still alive, so obviously tonight, I did my job right."

"So that's all that kiss was to you?" His words felt like knives in my heart, and I placed my hands on the back of the other armchair to steady myself. "Part of a job?"

"Maybe." He tilted his head, challenging me. "Why?"

"It just..." I swallowed and looked down, gathering the courage to say it. Once I did, I looked back up at him, trying to sound confident and cool—even though I felt the exact opposite. "It felt like more than that to me."

"Hm." He took out his knife and started rotating it in his hands. "What did it feel like to you?"

I almost blurted out that it was the most intense kiss —no, the most intense *experience*—I'd ever had in my life. But he was acting so blasé about it. So I stopped myself.

I couldn't bear my soul to him only to have him crush it in return.

But how could a kiss like that have been one-sided? It couldn't have been. If it were, then Noah had gone into the wrong profession. Because that kiss was Oscar worthy.

But admitting what I truly felt and finding out that it was just an act for him—his "playing his part" to keep me safe—would make me look pathetic and desperate. So I needed to be cool about this. I needed to let him know that the kiss meant something to me, but not *so* much that if it meant nothing to him, things would be weird between us for the rest of the hunt.

Why was it always so easy to be cool around guys who were my friends, but so difficult when I felt more? This was why I'd never had a serious boyfriend. Because the minute I actually had feelings for a guy, I turned into the biggest loser on the planet.

But the longer I stalled, the more awkward this was becoming. I needed to say something. Now.

"It meant something to me," I said simply. "I felt something between us." I shrugged, knowing I also needed to give him an out in case he didn't feel the same way—which was the possibility I was bracing myself for. "But if you didn't, that's cool. I'd just rather know so it doesn't happen again."

He said nothing for a few seconds—he just watched me with eyes so intense that I wanted to melt into the floor. My heart pounded a million beats a second, and I needed him to *say something* so this silence between us could end.

"I kissed you to keep the demon away from you," he finally said. "But you're right—there were other ways I could have done that. Ways that wouldn't have confused you. I promise it won't happen again."

My heart fell to the floor. "So it meant nothing to you," I said, sounding as hollow as I felt.

"You're a human," he said—as if I needed reminding. "I'm a shifter. Someday I'll imprint on a shifter, she'll imprint back on me, and we'll become mates. You and I could never work. Kissing you was a mistake, and I promise it won't happen again. You have my word."

My breath caught in my chest when he said that kissing me was a *mistake*. There were a lot of ways he could have told me he didn't return my feelings... but that was unnecessarily harsh.

Tears welled in my eyes, and I swallowed, unsure if I'd be able to speak without crying.

But I had to. I needed to leave this room with my dignity still intact.

"Thank you for your honesty," I said, somehow managing to force the tears down. "I'm going to bed. I'll see you for training tomorrow."

I didn't wait for his response.

Instead, I turned on my heel, the first tears rolling down my face as I hurried into the bedroom and slammed the door shut behind me.

SAGE

I tried to take my time in the shower, since Raven and Noah clearly needed to talk about what had happened between them at the bar. The suite was big, but it wasn't *so* big that any of the rooms were outside my range of hearing. The running shower water was as close as I could get to drowning them out to give them privacy.

When I came out of the bathroom, Raven was curled up in the bed in tears.

Crap. I was *not* good at dealing with crying girls. I'd been born and raised into a pack of fierce wolves, and I was the beta of the Montgomery pack—the second most dominant wolf in the pack. The submissives were the ones who provided comfort whenever a fellow pack member was upset. My pack mates came to me for leadership and motivation, not for comfort.

To say that I was unprepared to deal with a crying human girl was the understatement of the century.

But here we were, so I had to try.

"Raven?" I said softly, sitting down on my side of the bed. I left as much room between us as possible, not wanting to intrude on her personal space. "Are you okay?"

"I'm fine." She sniffed and sat up. Her cheeks were red and her eyes were puffy—she looked far from fine.

I shifted uncomfortably. "Is this about Noah?" I asked.

"No." She looked down at the bed, not meeting my eyes.

It was a lie. I couldn't say for sure—I couldn't smell lies like I could smell fear or sadness—but *something* had happened during the conversation they'd just had that made her come to the room crying by herself.

She smoothed her hair and wound it around her finger. "I've just been through a lot recently, and I think it's all catching up at once," she said, her voice wobbly and unsure. "I'm going to get ready for bed and go to sleep. I'll feel better in the morning."

She hurried to the bathroom and locked the door behind her.

I had no idea what was going on, but I marched out of the bedroom to find Noah, determined to find out.

Noah was sprawled out on one of the big armchairs near the fireplace, staring emptily into the flames. He looked broken and distraught—the same way he'd looked when I'd met him for the first time at that sketchy underground shifter bar in LA.

He glanced at me when I walked in, disappointment filling his eyes.

Had he expected me to be Raven?

"Patio," I said, pointing to the door that led outside. While human hearing wasn't as good as shifter hearing, Raven would probably be able to hear us from the bedroom—but she wouldn't be able to hear us from the patio. "Now."

He pushed himself out of the chair and followed me outside, looking dazed as he walked.

Whatever had happened between him and Raven must have thrown him for a real loop. And while I wasn't an expert at comforting, I was good at talking sense into people and advising them on how to fix whatever they'd messed up.

Once we were both outside, I shut the door tight,

making sure there was no chance Raven could overhear. Then I turned to Noah, who had his hands on the balcony and was gazing forlornly out over the skyline of the city.

I'd come out here under the assumption that he was leading Raven on. I was prepared to tell him to stop playing with her heart, because it could screw up our mission. But judging by the tortured expression in his eyes, he was just as upset as she was.

This was more of a mess than I'd anticipated.

I sat down on one of the seats and made myself comfortable, preparing to be out there for a while.

"You kissed Raven at the bar." I figured it was best to start by laying out the facts. "Now you're brooding out here and she's crying in the bedroom."

He stiffened when I said she was crying—as if the thought of it physically hurt him.

"What's going on between the two of you?" I asked.

He turned to face me, pure torment in his eyes. "I imprinted on her," he said in wonderment, as if he didn't quite believe it himself.

"What?" I looked at him like he was crazy. Because that's exactly what that statement was. Crazy. "You couldn't have," I said. "That's impossible."

"I know," he said. "But I did." He walked toward me, his steps as sure as ever, and sat down in the seat across from me. "I've felt a pull toward her since the moment I saw her on the Pier. I didn't think much of it until we brought her back to the compound. Because the more time I spent around her, the more drawn to her I was. So I figured I'd kiss her and get it out of my system. But you walked in before I could. In the pool house. Remember?"

"Of course," I said, thinking back to it. Her back had been against the wall, his arms pinning her in place. It had been clear what had been about to happen.

I'd gone there to bring Raven back to my room so she could find some clothes to borrow. She'd pulled herself away from Noah to come with me, and during that time, I'd figured it was only fair to tell her about the imprinting and mating process. It didn't seem right to let her get involved with Noah without knowing the facts beforehand. Also, since she was tagging along on our mission, I didn't want there to be any unnecessary drama between them.

"After she learned about imprinting and mating, she told me we needed to keep things professional between us," he continued. "I agreed, because it made sense. But it didn't make the pull I felt toward her go away."

"That's why you've been so snippety around her," I realized. "You've been frustrated."

"I guess." He shrugged. "I was trying to respect her

wishes, because I didn't want to hurt her. But when I saw that demon hanging all over her at the bar, looking at her like he wanted to eat her alive… I don't know what came over me. I just had this feeling that she was *mine* and I was going to show him that the best way I knew how. So I kissed her. And when I did…"

"You imprinted on her," I finished his sentence.

"Yep."

I stared at him, not believing it. "But she's a human," I said. "You're a shifter. You *can't* have imprinted on her. It's not possible." I knew I'd already said it, but I had to repeat it. Because it was true. There'd never been any accounts of shifters imprinting on anyone other than other shifters… ever.

"I know that," he said. "But I also know what happened. I imprinted on her. She's even used the empathy bond between us."

"Are you sure?" I asked. "I mean, neither of us ever told her about the empathy bond…" The connection between shifters when they imprinted and mated—the empathy bond and soul bond, retrospectively—was private between shifters. It gave mates an advantage in battle. Not even other types of supernaturals knew the details about it. So while I liked Raven, obviously it wasn't something we'd shared with her, since she was human.

"I'm sure," he said. "The first time she did it was when Leia was deciding which one of us should take the truth potion. Raven knew I didn't want to take it, but she also knew that if she volunteered, Leia would turn her down and choose me anyway. So Raven tapped into the empathy bond and gave me the feeling that I should volunteer, which would then make Leia choose Raven. I felt that Raven was comfortable taking the truth potion —she *wanted* to do it, since she had nothing to hide. So that's why I volunteered."

"Are you *sure* she used the empathy bond?" I was skeptical—it seemed unlikely that Raven magically knew about the existence of the secret shifter imprint bond. "Couldn't you have had that idea yourself? And you're telling yourself it was the empathy bond because you have feelings for her and *wish* you could imprint on her?"

"It wasn't a wish," he said stubbornly. "She connected with me through the empathy bond. You've never imprinted, so it's tough for you to understand. But I know what I felt."

I jolted back at his words. The reminder that I'd never imprinted on anyone was a sore subject, and hearing it said like that—like it made me incapable of understanding this important shifter experience—stung.

Probably because I wanted more than anything to find my mate.

Not all shifters my age were mated, but they'd at least imprinted on one or two others by now. The longer I went without imprinting, the more and more frustrated I got that it seemed like I would never have a mate.

"Sorry." Noah frowned when he realized he'd upset me. "I didn't mean to be harsh. But imprinting is something you can't understand until you feel it. I could feel *her*. She projected her desires upon me, and I knew what to do. And she did it again when we first got back to the hotel, when we were discussing using her as bait. I was prepared to lie and tell her that what she did wasn't helpful. I wanted to keep her safe. But I got this strong feeling from her that she needed me to be honest with her. So I was. That's why I was wrangled into giving into this crazy plan of hers at all."

"Okay." I paused, taking a few seconds to absorb everything he said.

Noah wasn't the type of guy to make something like this up. If he was telling me he'd imprinted on Raven, it was the truth. And he looked so torn up about it that I could tell he needed a friend more than ever. So I had to try to help him—even though I had no idea what to make of this, either.

"So, you imprinted on a human," I said, feeling like it was as good of a start as ever. "The question is—how?"

"I have no idea," he said. "I was hoping you might know something that might help explain."

"I'm as baffled by this as you are," I said honestly. "It shouldn't be possible."

"But it happened." He shrugged, as if he still couldn't believe it.

"I know." I sat back in the chair and took a deep breath. I'd always been particularly interested in imprinting, since it was something I wanted to happen to me more than anything. But there were literally *no* instances that I knew of when a shifter had imprinted on someone who wasn't a shifter. "Maybe you'll find an answer in Avalon," I said, since it was all I could come up with right now. "If anyone might know something, it's an angel."

"Annika's a new angel," Noah pointed out. "She thought she was human up until a few months ago."

It always amazed me that Noah was on first name basis with the Earth Angel. According to him, the Earth Angel wasn't one for prestigious titles, but still. It was pretty cool.

"She still might be able to help," I said. "And if she can't, there are others on Avalon. Vampires. Some of them have lived for centuries—maybe one of them will know something."

"Maybe," he said. "But I need you to promise you won't say anything to Raven."

"Why?" I asked, but the answer hit me quickly. "Never mind—I get it. You want to be the first one to tell her. Duh."

"No." Steely determination filled his eyes. "I don't plan on telling her at all."

"What?" I shook my head, sure he must be joking. "No. You have to tell her."

"I don't have to do anything," he said.

"But… you *imprinted* on each other," I said. "She needs to know."

"We didn't imprint on each other," he said. "I imprinted on her. There's a difference."

"What are you talking about?" I asked. "Imprinting is always a two-way street."

"It's a two-way street between shifters," he said. "Shifters can imprint—humans can't."

"So what... you think she didn't imprint back on you?"

He glanced down at his feet, his features twisted as if his heart had just been ripped out of his chest. He got a grip on himself a second later, but it was obvious—Noah was in serious pain over this.

I felt awful for him. "After everything you went through in the Vale, you deserve happiness," I said. "Why would you risk throwing that away by not telling her the truth?"

"You might think I deserve happiness, but apparently the universe disagrees," he said. "Because when you were in the shower, I asked Raven what it felt like for her when we kissed. She said she felt something, but that if I didn't, she was cool with that as long as we agreed not to let it happen again."

"She said that?" I didn't believe it. "Or is that how you perceived it?"

"Those actual words came out of her mouth," he said. "So I know she didn't imprint back. If she did, she wouldn't be 'cool with it if I didn't feel something, as long as it didn't happen again.' Because just *knowing* that it can't happen again is eating me up inside. She's not experiencing what I am. Trust me."

"Hold up," I interrupted, holding a hand up to stop him from brooding about this any further. "Why, exactly, can't it happen again?"

He stared at me like I was an idiot. "Because she didn't imprint back," he said.

"But she said she felt something," I said. "Maybe she just said the rest to soften the blow in case you didn't feel anything back. So why deny your feelings for her? Why not let it play out and see what happens?"

"You obviously haven't done as much thinking about this as I have," he said.

"Obviously not." I sat forward and clasped my hands together on my lap. "So please, enlighten me. Because right now it just seems like you're creating drama where there doesn't need to be any. And really, the last thing the three of us need right now is more drama."

"I imprinted on her, and she didn't imprint back," he said. "There's no way that can end well. So nothing can happen between us."

"Are you forgetting that she's crying in her bed now?" I asked, pointing my thumb toward the room. "She wouldn't be crying if she doesn't care."

"Let me spell it out for you," he said. "Humans can't imprint back, which means it would be impossible for us to mate. You and I both know that unmated shifters can imprint on more than one person at once. So I could be imprinted on her, we could decide to date, and then I could imprint on someone else—a shifter who *could* be my mate. Even if Raven and I loved each other, it would be my instinct to choose a potential shifter mate bond over a one-sided human imprint bond. Raven would be getting herself invested in a relationship doomed to fail. I don't want to put her through that."

"I think you're jumping to a lot of conclusions…" I said.

"I'm thinking through the possible scenarios," he shot back at me. "That's the one that's most likely."

"And what if you're wrong?" I asked. "What if she *did* imprint back on you?"

"Then she'd *never* be safe." His eyes were hard—I could tell he really *had* thought about this. "You know how most shifters are. They'd think it was disgusting for a shifter to imprint on a human. She'd be a constant target for being such an anomaly. I'd be cursing her to a lifetime of danger, and she deserves better than that."

"You're wrong." My frustration with Noah's stubbornness was turning into anger, and I clenched my fists in an attempt to rein in my emotions. "She deserves a *choice*."

"None of it will matter, anyway," he said. "Because

once we get to Avalon, she's going to go through the Angel Trials, become a Nephilim, and get her mom back. She'll find someone who will be able to give himself to her completely—another Nephilim, or maybe even a vampire. She'll find happiness. And I'm going to give that to her by letting her go—now, before anything can start between us."

I narrowed my eyes, waiting for him to add something more. Waiting for him to say that he couldn't let her go so easily.

But he didn't.

He was apparently determined with his decision.

"You're afraid," I said, since it was the only reason why I could think he was being so stubborn about this.

"I'm not afraid." His eyes were hard—the emotion and torment from earlier gone. "I'm being realistic."

"You're not going to budge on this," I realized. "Are you?"

"No," he said. "I've made my decision, and it's final."

"Fine," I said. "But I still think she should know."

"So what?" He sat straighter. "Are you going to tell her?" He watched me in challenge, daring me to go behind his back and tell her his secret.

"Of course not," I said. "You're my hunting partner—my *friend*. I might not agree with you, but I'd never betray you like that. So I won't say anything to Raven."

"Thank you." He let out a breath he'd been holding and relaxed into his chair. "It's the best thing for her. You'll see."

"Maybe." I shrugged. "But we still have three more demons to kill on this hunt. Maybe between now and the time we get to Avalon, you'll come to your senses and tell Raven the truth. She might just be a human, but she's smart, fiery, determined, and kind."

"I know." He closed his eyes and pressed his fingers against them, taking a deep breath before opening them again. "I've spent more time with her than you have. Obviously I know all this about her by now."

"Then you should also know that people like her don't come around often," I said. "You were *lucky* to imprint with her. I just hope you don't throw that away."

FLINT

I was shooting pool in a local supernatural bar, taking out my anger on the billiard balls as I recalled the phone conversation I'd had earlier that day with Sage.

She'd updated me on how the hunt was progressing —along with letting me know about the attack from the coyotes in Texas. I'd feigned outrage, swearing that the coyotes would pay for attacking a member of the Montgomery pack.

When I'd asked her where she was heading next, she'd told me she couldn't tell me—that she wasn't telling *anyone*. She'd said that now that someone was after her, the less people who knew where she was, the better. I'd insisted she could trust me, but she'd refused to give me any information apart from the fact that they intended on leaving New Orleans later tonight.

My sister was smart—I had to give her that.

Luckily, I had another ace up my sleeve. Because while Sage and Noah both wore cloaking rings, the human they were traveling with was traceable. The human had also left the sandals she'd been wearing when she'd gotten to the Montgomery compound in the pool house. All I had to do was bring one of those shoes to the Devereux mansion tomorrow and have Amber do a tracking spell to see where the trio ended up next.

Once I pinned down their location, I'd work out another plan to capture Sage.

I'd just shot two balls into the holes at once when I spotted a familiar face in the corner of my eye.

Azazel.

His eyes were brown instead of red, his teeth looked human, and his scent was hidden. Hiding his demonic features from supernaturals must have been a *very* expensive cloaking spell. But no one other than me knew what he looked like, so no one else was paying him any attention.

He was standing off to the side of the bar, and from the way he was watching me, I knew he was there to speak to me. He looked around his surroundings in wonderment—taking in everything from the copious selection of drinks behind the bar, the elegance of the furniture, and the everyday clothes people were wearing.

Mara had told me that Hell hadn't advanced like Earth. Before the demons destroyed all their resources in the war that ended their realm, Hell had resembled our Dark Ages. Now Hell was scorched to oblivion. She and Azazel were both impressed by the technological advancements on Earth—by the luxuries we took for granted everyday.

Supernaturals preferred to depend on magic instead of machines, so I supposed technology was one of the few good things that humans had provided this world. Without humans, we might have still been stuck in the Dark Ages, too.

I looked around for Mara, but she wasn't there. Looked like it was just going to be Azazel and me.

I couldn't say I was looking forward to it. But I had to do what I had to do.

I handed off my pool stick to one of the other guys in the pack. "I have some business to attend to," I told him. "You can play for me from here."

He did as I said, not questioning me as I walked away.

As usual, the bar was full of the most common type of supernatural—low powered witches. There were a few rogue vampires thrown in as well. Vampires all smelled metallic, but even if their scent didn't give them away, it would have been easy to spot them. Because most of them were surrounded by witches.

For witches with low magical aptitude, getting turned by a vampire was their best chance of gaining the power they lacked. Vampires rarely turned others—they'd suffer consequences if a vampire they sired lost control of their bloodlust—but that didn't stop weak witches from trying.

However, while the vampires were powerful, the wolves of the Montgomery pack were the most powerful supernaturals in the bar. Besides Azazel, of course.

The other patrons stepped clear of my path as I made my way toward the greater demon.

"Flint," he said once I reached him.

"Sir." I figured that was the best way to address him in public, since others would recognize his true name if I spoke it.

"I have news." As always, the greater demon got straight to the point. "Where can we speak privately?"

"The booths in the back," I said. "The drinks cost triple the price back there, but each booth is enchanted with a sound blocking spell to provide privacy."

Magical extras were one of the perks of coming to

supernatural bars, along with how they served blood for vampires and didn't question it when shifters ordered our meat extra rare.

A waitress approached us the moment we situated ourselves in one of the back booths. She had a faint, sweet smell to her—she was a low-powered witch. Luckily for her, she had stunning good looks to make up for her lack of power. I would have tried to have a bit of fun with her if I wasn't already imprinted on Mara.

She smiled at both of us, but focused on me once she realized Azazel wasn't acknowledging her existence. "There's a one drink minimum per hour to sit in the private booths," she said what I already knew. "Do you know what you want to order, or do you need time to check out the menu?"

"Two Johnnie Walker Blues," I said, since I knew from previous conversations with Azazel that scotch was his drink of choice. "On me."

She returned with our drinks a minute later, letting us know that she'd leave us in private for the next hour unless we signaled to her that we needed anything.

Then she left, giving us the space we desired, and I braced myself for the news Azazel was going to drop on me next.

FLINT

I pulled the curtain, not wanting anyone to try reading our lips, and looked at Azazel to begin.

As the alpha, I was used to leading conversations. But since this was Azazel I was sitting across from, I held back, waiting for him to start. It felt unnatural to defer to someone else, but I had to do what I had to do to ensure safety for the pack, and to be able to mate with Mara.

The greater demon raised his glass to take a sip, and I mirrored his actions. "Delicious," he said after tasting the scotch. He swirled the amber liquid around in the glass, looking at it in appreciation. "The delicacies available on Earth haven't ceased to amaze me."

"I'm glad you're pleased," I replied.

He nodded and took another sip of scotch, pausing to savor it. "I'm sure you're wondering why I came to you tonight," he started, and I nodded for him to continue. "How is the progress coming with your sister?"

"Sage is still in New Orleans," I answered honestly. "Once she leaves the rougarou territory, I'll do everything in my power to pin down her next location and capture her."

"You don't know where she's going next?" he asked.

"Not yet," I said. "But I have a plan."

He leveled his gaze with mine, the side of his lip turning up into a knowing smirk. "Your plan won't work," he said surely.

"What are you talking about?" I narrowed my eyes, tightening my grasp around my glass of scotch. "No one knows the details of this plan but me."

"You intend on go to Amber of the Devereux witches and ask her to use a tracking spell to find your sister," he said. "The item you intend on bringing with you to track her is a shoe."

I took a sharp breath inward, terror racing through my veins. It wasn't my exact plan—he hadn't mentioned the human—but it was close enough to set me on edge. "How did you know?" I asked. Because if Azazel knew that, did he also know I'd been lying about why Sage was gone? Did he know that the story about Sage and Noah being lovers and running off to be together was false?

"I have my ways," he said smugly, sitting back in his booth.

"What sort of ways?" I asked. Because I hadn't told *anyone* my plan.

Which meant Azazel must have read my mind.

I didn't think demons were telepathic. But if Azazel somehow was, then I was in deep trouble.

"Let's just say that I have some psychic help on my side," he said. "An ally as powerful as Rosella of the Haven. And while your plan will fail, I have information that will locate your sister."

I relaxed at the realization that Azazel didn't have mind-reading capabilities. But if he had a psychic as powerful as Rosella as an ally—which it seemed like he did—he and the other demons were a bigger threat than ever.

It was a good thing I was making this alliance between him and the Montgomerys. Once the demons unleashed their full power upon the Earth and took over the planet for themselves, my pack mates were going to be grateful for my foresight that kept them alive. *Including* my sister.

If Azazel could help me locate Sage, I was going to take it.

"What do you want in return for this information?" I asked.

"Flint," he said with a smile. "I'm doing you a favor. Why do you assume I want anything in return?"

He was a demon. Of *course* he wanted something in return.

But I knew better than to say that.

"I'm sorry, Your Grace." I lowered my eyes as I used his preferred title—since lowering them stopped me from rolling them. "I shouldn't have assumed your intentions."

"No." He laughed. "You absolutely should have."

At least my instincts weren't totally off.

I looked at him to continue, not surprised that Azazel wasn't giving me something from the goodness of his heart.

"Of course I want something in return," he said. "You see, I believe you're going to stand by your word and go through with the blood binding ceremony—you love Mara too much to refuse. And I believe you'll command your pack to follow in your footsteps. I believe you so much that I didn't ask you to make a blood oath that you'd follow through on your word." He sat forward and rested his elbows on the table, staring at me straight on.

"But despite my faith in you, there's one wild card left— your sister. If you can't get your sister back here before the fortnight is up, I have no idea what you'll do. And that lack of predictability is a problem for me, Flint."

I took a sip of scotch, stalling. Because Azazel was right. If I couldn't get Sage back in time, I wasn't sure what I'd do regarding the blood binding ceremony.

I was just focused on retrieving her so it wouldn't come down to that decision.

Azazel apparently didn't expect me to deny his statement, because he continued without faltering.

"At the same time, your dedication to your sister shows loyalty, and I can't blame you for loyalty," he said. "Especially since you're Mara's future mate, which means your loyalty will be to her—and thus, to the demons."

"I will do everything in my power to keep Mara safe," I promised.

"I know." Azazel smiled. "Which is why I'm offering you this deal. You see, my psychic doesn't just know which cities your sister will head to next. She also knows which of those cities you'll be most likely to capture her in. I'll tell you the name of that city. In exchange, you'll make a blood oath with me, promising you'll go through with the blood binding ceremony— and that you'll command your pack to go through the ceremony as well—whether your sister is retrieved in time or not."

My stomach flipped at the implication of his proposal. My instinct was to say no, since I didn't want to promise anything that might bind me to betraying my sister, but I held my tongue. I had to control my impulses. I didn't want to say anything I might regret.

"You understand that while I do command my pack, I can't *force* them to do anything against their will," I said instead. "Correct?"

"I understand that," Azazel said. "I also know you can't make a blood oath for any actions except your own. I've been around for a while—I understand the rules for these things. But you *can* do everything in your power to get your pack to heed your advice. The magic of the blood oath will know if you don't." He paused, as if letting it sink in. The way my blood would turn on me and burn me from the inside out if I went against an oath. An oath so powerful that its magic could kill even an angel in Heaven if that angel went against it. "So… there's my offer," he continued. "What do you say? Will you take it or leave it?"

I paused, thinking it over. I always avoided entering into blood oaths unless they were completely necessary. They were too permanent, and I liked to be able to change my mind when it suited me.

But I needed to know Sage's next location. Knowing could be the difference between getting her back in time or not. Between her safety or her being killed by the demons.

"Oh, and Flint?" Azazel added, and I looked to him to continue. "If you refuse to make this blood oath, I'll assume you've been lying about your loyalty this entire time, and my offer will be off. I'll find another pack to blood bind with me, you won't mate with Mara, and, well… you know what the demons plan to do to shifters who aren't bound to us. Right?"

Of course I knew. The demons planned on exterminating all supernaturals from Earth. The only exceptions would be the shifters who pledged loyalty by binding themselves to the demons.

If I didn't go through with this blood oath, the Montgomerys would surely be first on Azazel's hit list.

I either had to risk losing my sister—which likely wouldn't happen, since he'd be giving me information I needed to find her—or risk losing everything.

It wasn't much of a choice. What I needed to do was clear.

"You have yourself a deal." I shifted my fingernail into a claw and made an incision in my palm, holding it out to the greater demon across from me. "I'm ready to make the blood oath."

RAVEN

*A*fter what had happened between Noah and me, I expected training the next day to be awkward, to say the least. Luckily, Sage joined in, which stopped any awkwardness from happening. Noah was all business—focused on teaching me as many defensive moves as possible before sunset—and Sage kept the conversation going the entire time with everyday chitchat.

Since supernaturals had humanoid forms—except for shifters in their animal forms—they had the same sensitive areas as humans. I learned all about the most effective body parts to strike in a fight—the eyes, nose, ears, neck, groin, knee, and legs. Noah had me reciting that and pretending to hit those areas so many times that I could sing the jingle I made up to remember it in my sleep. Besides their strength, supernaturals had a higher tolerance for pain than humans, and they healed faster. So I wouldn't be able to do *much* damage. I was learning this to stun a potential attacker, break free of their hold, and hopefully buy myself time before help came.

We practiced getting out of so many holds that I felt like a human pretzel.

Of course, whenever I practiced getting out of a hold, I practiced with Sage—not with Noah. Noah only touched me when absolutely necessary.

He was acting like my skin was poisoned, and touching me burned him. And when he talked to me, he was straight to the point and devoid of emotions. Like talking to a robot.

I hadn't thought things could get worse between us than him constantly making me feel useless and unwanted... but I was wrong. At least before, he acknowledged my existence.

This lack of emotion was far, far worse.

By the time we finished up for the day, I was drenched in sweat and every muscle in my body was screaming out in pain.

I spent extra long in the shower, glad to have time to myself. Right now, I needed space from Noah. But that wasn't going to happen. So until we got to Avalon,

I was just going to have to deal with being around him.

When I came out of the shower, Noah and Sage had already packed up our stuff. Once they showered, we'd head out to the Voodoo Queen to pick up my cloaking ring and have her do a scrying spell to locate the nearest demon.

Once we knew the location of the demon, we'd head out on the road.

After all, there was no reason to waste time sleeping in the hotel when we could switch off sleeping in the car.

Everything went smoothly with the Voodoo Queen. She did the scrying spell to discover our next destination— Charleston, South Carolina.

It took us all night to drive to Charleston, and we finally arrived in the morning. Charleston seemed like a cool little city—I would have liked to spend time there if we hadn't been on a hunt to kill three more demons as quickly as possible.

Much to Sage's dismay, there were no Ritz-Carlton's in Charleston, but we found a cool luxury boutique hotel to stay in. She booked the biggest suite available.

We had the same sleeping arrangement as New Orleans —Sage and I sharing the king bed in the bedroom, and Noah on the couch in the living room.

Charleston was apparently a town known for supernatural activity, and Amber pointed us in the direction of the most powerful witch circle in the city. The witches in the circle lived in a quaint townhouse walking distance from where we were staying downtown. From the looks of all the timeless antiques inside, the house had been in their family for generations. The leader of the circle—Yasmine—did a scrying spell and located the demon at a popular bar nearby.

Using me as bait went *exactly* as planned. Noah stood back, and Sage and I situated ourselves at the bar. As expected, the demon gravitated to me soon after we sat down. Again, he was in the form of a generic-looking man in his twenties. Since I couldn't see past his supernatural glamour, Sage pinched me—the signal we'd created—to let me know he was the target.

It was still a mystery why the demons were so attracted to me, or what they wanted with me. It was something that was constantly bothering me. Especially because I wondered if my missing memories had something to do with it. But since Sage and Noah didn't have answers, I tried not to mention it much.

I'd worry about it once I reached Avalon.

For now, we had demon hunting to focus on.

Just like in New Orleans, Sage and I flirted with the demon and eventually left the bar with him. Unlike in New Orleans, we didn't give him enough time to pull us into a random alley.

We pulled him into an alley first—one that *we'd* selected ahead of time.

He was so surprised by Sage's supernatural strength that I don't think he processed what was happening before Noah came up behind him with his slicer. In what looked like less than a second, Noah stabbed his knife into the demon's heart, crumbling him to dust.

Noah stood over the pile of ash and admired his handiwork. "That took us less than twelve hours," he said as he picked up one of the demon teeth and stashed it in his pocket. "If Yasmine can find the location of another demon tonight, we can hit the road without even spending the night here."

"Was that your fastest hunt yet?" I asked.

"Maybe." Noah shrugged. "I don't time them."

That went against what he said by announcing it took less than twelve hours, but whatever. I was so *over* arguing with him.

"Yes," Sage said with a smile. "It definitely was."

"Great." I gave her a small curtsey and glanced

toward what was left of the demon. "I'm glad to be of service."

Then I turned around and led the way back to Yasmine's, still smiling as Sage and Noah followed behind.

Eight demons down, two more to go.

RAVEN

$\mathcal{I}$t was another overnight drive before we arrived at our next destination—Nashville. The lack of a solid night of sleep was starting to catch up with me, but I didn't complain.

I could sleep once I got to Avalon and found my mom.

Until then, we'd hunt.

We were also bracing ourselves for another attack like the one from the coyotes. We still had no idea who they were working for or why they'd wanted Sage, but they'd yet to make another strike. It was a good thing, but none of us counted on it lasting. We doubted we'd be *that* lucky. So next time they attacked, we'd keep one of them alive and use truth potion to uncover their motives and get them to tell us who they were working for.

But while we remained on the lookout for anyone who might be after us, all we could do now was stay focused on the hunt.

Like in Charleston, there were no Ritz's in Nashville. So Sage used Google during the drive there to research the best hotel in the city and book a room. We didn't bother to unpack, since hopefully we wouldn't be staying for long.

The witches in the area lived in a suburb outside of Nashville called Brentwood. Sage gave them a call and was able to book us an appointment for that evening. I was quickly learning that the supernatural community was nocturnal and tended to do business at night. Probably because of the vampires.

At first I hoped that the evening appointment meant we'd have time to rest. But I had no such luck.

Because Noah decided it was time for me to practice using the knife I kept in my boot. And unlike last time, Sage wouldn't be joining. She was going to drive to a car dealership to replace the beat up truck we'd taken from the coyotes with a brand new Range Rover.

Which meant Noah and I would be training alone.

We didn't have a patio like at the Ritz, so he pushed the living room furniture to the edges of the room so we could practice in there. There was enough space in the center of the room so we could hopefully train without breaking anything.

Like always, he was focused and got straight to business. He kept his distance and tried to avoid skin on skin contact whenever possible. But he didn't succeed all the time.

Whenever his skin touched mine, I could have sworn I saw *pain* swirl in his eyes.

It hurt every time, because whenever I touched him, I didn't want to let go. His touch thrilled me and sent warmth through my body, making me want more. I craved his touch like an addict waiting for their next fix.

But all I had to do was look at him to see that he clearly felt exactly the opposite way. He looked like he couldn't bear touching me. He was just dealing with it because he had to.

To make everything worse, I was having a hard time focusing, so it was taking me longer to learn than it should have. This frustrated him, and created a circle of anger that I didn't think I could escape from.

We were an hour into training when I couldn't handle the tension between us anymore. I just wanted this to *end*.

I broke out of his hold, reached for the knife in my

boot, twirled to face him, and held the knife up to his neck. Adrenaline fueled me the entire time.

I was just as shocked as he was when I realized that I'd done the move we'd been working on correctly.

"Not bad." He pushed the knife down and took a step back.

"Not bad?" I asked, the knife dangling by my side. "I thought that was pretty awesome."

He said nothing in response, instead just launching into telling me what we'd be working on next. Anger swirled in my stomach, getting stronger and stronger until it filled my chest, feeling like it was about to explode.

"Noah," I said his name strongly but firmly, interrupting him as he explained something I was having trouble focusing on anyway.

He paused, looking stunned by the interruption.

It was the first time he'd looked at me—truly *looked* at me—since the kiss that had ruined everything.

And now that I had his attention, I had to speak my peace.

"I hate the way things have been between us since New Orleans." I tried to keep my voice steady, despite the fact that it terrified me to be so open about my emotions.

He gave me a once over, and then closed himself off again. "I don't know what you're talking about," he said.

"Come on." I rolled my eyes, rushing to continue before he could respond. "Listen—I get that the kiss meant nothing to you. It was part of our act to hunt the demon. That's fine. I'm fine with that." It was a lie, but whatever. If I needed to lie about my feelings to save face, then so be it. "But I'm *not* fine with you treating me like I'm less than human."

"I'm helping you learn how to fight—like you wanted me to do in the first place," he said. "How is that treating you like you're less than human?"

"You're acting like I barely exist!" I said. "When I talk to you, it feels like I'm talking to a robot."

He took a step closer, looking at me so intensely that my entire body felt like it turned to jelly. It took all of my effort to remember to hold onto the handle of my knife so it didn't drop to the floor.

Was he about to kiss me?

Because I recognized that look—it was the same one he'd given me in the bar in New Orleans, right before he'd kissed me.

Kiss me, I thought, trying to use the same manifestation technique that I had when we'd been captured by the rougarou. I put everything I could into the thought, trying to let him feel my desire and know that if he felt the same, he shouldn't hide it anymore. *Kiss me, and we can finally stop pretending that this pull we feel toward each other doesn't exist.*

His eyes dilated, like he was dazed by my very presence. We moved closer and closer together, like magnets that couldn't resist each other anymore.

Joy spread through my stomach at the realization that whatever I was doing was working. He was going to kiss me again.

But then he stepped back, looking away from me to stare out the window.

The joy I'd felt dissipated in an instant. It was like one moment he was there with me, and the next he'd checked out completely.

"Training's done for the day," he said, not looking at me as he spoke.

"What?" The pain of being rejected—again—sliced my heart in two.

"Because I said so," he said. "Go to your room and get some rest." He looked me over, like he was inspecting me and didn't like what he was seeing. "From the looks of you, you need it."

*S*age pulled me out of bed a few hours later, and the three of us got in the brand new Range Rover and headed to the suburbs. The witches of Nashville did the scrying spell for the demon and located him in one of the most popular bars in Nashville.

"Were the first five demons you hunted always in such crowded areas, too?" I asked as we hopped into the car to head back downtown. Sage was driving, Noah was in the passenger seat, and I took the back. I directed the question to Sage, since Noah and I were doing most of our communication through her these past two days.

"Yep," she said. "The most challenging part of the hunt has always been tracking them and waiting until they're in a place where we can kill them without drawing attention to ourselves. Until you came along, of course."

I smiled at the reminder that I truly was helping them with their mission.

"I wonder why they're always in such packed places," I said, fiddling with the clunky black cloaking ring I now wore on my middle finger. It was big and heavy, and I didn't think I'd ever get used to it. "Maybe to avoid hunters like us?"

"They're searching for something." Noah stared straight ahead, not turning around to look at me as he spoke. "We already know there's something about you that the demons want. Whatever that thing is, it must be rare. So it's a numbers game. In crowded areas there are more people, and if there are more people, the demons are more likely to find what they're looking for."

"Me," I said. "Or someone like me."

"Yep." He didn't bother saying anything more.

"Plus, people are drinking in bars," Sage chimed in. "It's easier to get a drunk person to follow you down an alley than a sober person."

"You'd think even a drunk person would know better than to follow a man they don't know down an alley," I muttered.

"Except demons aren't normal men—or women," Sage said. "Demons have a strange effect on humans.

They make them do things they otherwise wouldn't. Bad things, daring things. They bring out a person's 'inner demon,' so to say. And from what I've seen, people who are drunk are easier for them to influence than people who are sober."

I thought back to when Eli had approached me at the bar on the Santa Monica Pier. It had been my twenty-first birthday, so I'd been drinking. While I was talking to him, I'd been getting red flags to walk away. But I'd also felt drawn to him. I'd ultimately made the decision to walk away, but I'd still talked to him for longer than I should have.

Could that be what Sage was talking about?

I wasn't sure, so I asked.

"Sounds about right," she said. "It's also why Joe was trying to get you to drink in New Orleans. He wanted to make it easier to influence you."

"Gross." I shuddered, glad I'd had the sense to turn down his offer.

"But props to you for being able to walk away from Eli at that bar," she added. "I don't think most humans would have been able to do that. It takes pure stubbornness to push past the will of a demon."

"Well, I'm nothing if not stubborn," I said.

"That's for sure," Noah muttered.

There he was—well, there was a *hint* of the snarky

guy I knew before the kiss made everything super weird between us.

"Hey." I pretended to be hurt, although really, I was just trying to bring back a sense of normalcy between us. "I think stubbornness is a good thing."

"Whatever." He shrugged and returned to pretending I didn't exist.

Sage tried to fill the silence with chatter. But it didn't come close to getting everything back to normal.

Because things between Noah and me would never go back to the way they were before, and it was about time I stopped hoping they would.

RAVEN

$\mathcal{B}$ack at the hotel, we changed and geared up to hunt the demon. Right before leaving, Sage and I both swished our mouths with vodka. We didn't swallow a drop, but smelling like vodka would help convince the demon that we'd been drinking.

It was a ten-minute walk from the hotel to the bar. The building was a three-floor monstrosity in the middle of the busiest street in the city. Each floor featured a different band, all of them playing country music. It was so packed that it was nearly impossible to walk without crashing into someone. The music was loud, the drinks were flowing, and the floor was sticky with spilled alcohol. I spotted at *least* three crowds of women out to celebrate bachelorette parties. In general, people were hooting and hollering and looked to be having the time of their lives. If my life were still normal, it might have even been the type of place I'd enjoy.

"I don't see our friend on the first floor," Noah said once we found ourselves a place to stand off to the side. "I'll do a complete sweep and then move up to the other two levels. Sage, you stay here with Raven and make sure our friend doesn't come down the stairs. If they do—"

"If they do, I'm sure they'll zero in on Raven, like the others have," Sage finished. "We'll keep them talking for long enough to allow you to come back down and find us. Now, go check the other floors. Send us a message once our friend is located, and we'll join you there and get into position."

He gave her a nod, glanced at me with an unreadable expression, and set off to locate the demon.

"He worries about you, you know," Sage said once he was gone.

"No, he doesn't." I scoffed and crossed my arms. "He hates me."

"He hates that he worries about you," she said. "But I promise he doesn't hate you. Far, far from it."

"What do you mean by that?" I turned to her, suddenly feeling like two normal girls out at a bar instead of a shifter and a—well, a whatever I was that the demons wanted so badly—out on a demon hunt. "Did he say something about me?"

Sadness crossed over her eyes—like she was sad for *me*. "It's not my place to get involved," she said, looking away from me before I could read any further into her expression. "I just thought it was obvious that he worries about you. He wasn't on edge like this before you joined us. Now, he feels an insane amount of pressure to make sure you don't get hurt. It's hard on him."

"Well, he has a funny way of showing it," I said, although Sage's words gave me hope that maybe all wasn't lost between Noah and me.

Then I remembered the way he'd been treating me recently, and I shoved that hope far down into a place where I couldn't reach it. I shoved it into the same place where I was hiding my fear for my mom, and my worry about what had happened to me when I thought I'd been in Europe.

But that wasn't good enough, so I shoved it down even deeper. Because I'd be able to think about my mom and Europe sometime in the future.

There was no point in pining for someone who was constantly annoyed by my mere existence.

Luckily, I didn't have much time to pine before Sage's phone lit up with a message. It was from Noah.

"I found our friend on level two," his recording

played back after Sage pressed play. "He's in the center of the bar—you'll see him when you get up here. I've assumed position on the stairs. We'll play it out just like Charleston. It'll be easy."

He hadn't needed to add that last part—we'd already decided to do the same thing we'd done in Charleston. There was no need to fix something that wasn't broken.

So why had he said it? It almost sounded like he was trying to reassure us that it was all going to go okay.

People only reassured other people when they *cared* about the other person.

Just like that, the hope that he might care about me started to slowly climb its way back into my heart.

But I had to push it down. We had a task to focus on.

So I nodded to Sage that I was ready, and together, the two of us headed upstairs to bait the demon.

$\mathcal{N}$oah waited at the top of the steps, but Sage and I walked past him, like we didn't know him. He ignored us as well.

Together, Sage and I walked arm in arm toward the bar. I let her lead me, since she was the one who could see through the demon's glamour. Once I knew who the demon was, I'd be able to see flashes of his red eyes, but I wouldn't be able to see through his glamour until then.

The bar was so packed that it was impossible for Sage and I to get past the rows of people to get a drink. Well, Sage probably could have used her supernatural strength to plow past them. But we were trying to blend in here and *not* clue the demon into the fact that she was dangerous. So she had to pretend she was as weak as everyone else.

Not like it mattered. Because as long as I was in the demon's line of sight, all we had to do was wait.

"Three, two, one…" Sage counted down.

"Excuse me," a man said from behind me, gently touching my elbow.

I turned around to face a guy in his twenties wearing a plaid button down shirt and jeans. With his all-American looks, he blended in perfectly with the country style of this city.

"Hi." I forced a smile at the same time that I saw the familiar flash of red in his eyes.

"You look like you could use some help getting the bartender's attention," he said, already raising his arm to flag a bartender down. "Can I buy you a drink?"

"Oh." I paused to glance at the bar and giggled. "I don't know. I've had a few already…" I made a show of counting on my fingers, as if trying to remember how many drinks I'd had so far that night.

The drunker the demon thought I was, the easier he'd think his job would be.

"You've had five," Sage said throwing in a giggle of her own. "Or six. I don't know. I've lost count."

"Sounds like you girls are already off to a good night," the demon said, holding his hand out to shake mine. "I'm John."

Apparently, he was being just as creative with his fake name as Joe.

"Rochelle." I gave him a fake name of my own and shook his hand, despite the fact that touching him made me want to cringe. "And this is my friend Sloan."

"Nice to meet you." He glanced at the bar, barely looking at Sage. "So, how about that drink?"

"I don't know." I stumbled slightly into Sage and grabbed her arm, pretending to be so drunk that I needed help standing. "It's getting *so* crowded here. We were thinking of checking out a bar closer to our hotel instead." I paused and looked "John" up and down, as if debating my next move. Then I smiled, tilted my head, and asked, "Wanna come?"

He smirked, as if he couldn't believe his luck. "Only if you let me buy you a drink once we get to the next bar," he said.

"Deal." I laughed—this time for *real,* since the joke would be on John once we never reached another bar.

The three of us headed toward the steps, Sage and I both stumbling a bit to keep up the ruse of being drunk. Noah moved away before we got there. He was now a few feet behind us, pretending to watch a sports game on one of the TVs. He didn't look at us once. No one would have had any clue that he knew us.

"So, what's the name of this bar you're taking me to?"

the demon asked as we made our way down the stairs. Lots of people were trying to get up and down, so I had to keep my hand on Sage's shoulder the entire time.

The demon kept his hand on me. Yuck.

"It's this little speakeasy our friends told us about," I improvised. "I don't know the name, but I know how to get there. It's really fun. I promise."

"Which way is it?" he asked. "Maybe I've heard of it."

"We turn right out of here and keep walking," I said. "Then it's down this little side street. I'll know it when I see it."

Sage, Noah, and I had chosen the side street ahead of time because it was a dead end, making it the perfect spot to slay a demon.

"Hm." He glanced around, looking hesitant. "I also know a cool place, but it's in the other direction. Are you girls up for some adventure first?"

No way. Any adventure that ended in coming face to face with Azazel got a definite *pass* from me.

"I don't know." I pouted in a way that I hoped looked drunkenly endearing. "My sister's at the bar we're going to, and I promised her we'd meet up with her soon…"

"Your sister?" The demon perked up the moment I mentioned my made-up sister. "A sorority sister or a blood sister?"

"Twin sister," I said, and his eyes lit up like he'd struck a jackpot.

His reaction was what I'd expected. Apparently, whatever the demons saw in me was genetic, since they'd hunted my mom too. I knew he wouldn't be able to resist two for the price of one.

"Two of you." He stared at me with hunger in his eyes. "Well, isn't it my lucky night?"

"It sure is." I beamed. "So, you'll come with us?"

"By all means." He motioned out of the bar. "Lead the way."

We walked until reaching a sky blue fire hydrant with flower art on it—the marker for the alley to turn down.

"It's just this way." I pointed, leading the way down the alley.

"Are you sure?" the demon asked. "It doesn't look like there's anything down there…"

"It's a *speakeasy*," I said playfully, sticking my tongue out to tease him. "Don't you know what a speakeasy is?"

"Honestly, no," he admitted.

At first I was surprised. But I supposed that since the demons had been locked in Hell for so many centuries, they would have missed out on a lot of human history.

"In the 1920s, during prohibition—when alcohol was

illegal—people still wanted to go out to bars and party," I started my brief history lesson as the three of us continued down the alley. "But they couldn't risk getting caught by the cops. So they created speakeasies—bars you couldn't find without knowing where they were ahead of time, because they were hidden in places like basements and alleys." I wasn't sure if it was true about alleys, but I threw it in for good measure since it fit with my story. "People needed special code words and knocks to get in. You'll see."

"You're pretty smart, aren't you?" he asked.

"I guess." I shrugged and looked away, then pointed down the next turn—the deserted alley that led to a dead end. "This way."

"You sure?" he asked, and then he turned to Sage, clearly doubting me. "Is she sure?" he asked her.

"We've been here before," Sage said. "This is definitely the right place."

I walked up to a rusty old door that looked like it hadn't been used in years and made a show out of knocking on it in a special way.

I only got in two knocks before Noah burst into the alley, slicer in hand.

The demon pulled out a dagger of his own, meeting Noah's blade in the air.

As they fought, I pressed myself against the wall,

knowing better to get stuck in the middle of it. Noah could handle this.

Then we'd be one tooth away from our final demon kill—and our entrance to Avalon.

But then someone else tore through the alley. A wolf. And not just any wolf—a shifter. I could tell because it was twice as big as an average, non-supernatural wolf. It was the same size as Noah and Sage when they turned.

Was it here to help us fight the demon?

Its eyes met mine for a second, and when they did, I saw them flash red. Like a demon.

"What?" Sage gasped, staring at the wolf like it was an alien. "It's not possible…"

The wolf jumped onto Sage before she could finish her thought, pinning her onto the ground while she was still in her human form. It raised its head and opened its jaw, looking ready to take a bite right out of Sage's neck. But Sage shifted into wolf form in the nick of time, using her own weight to roll over her opponent and gain an advantage.

They were moving around each other too quickly for me to help. If I tried anything, I'd likely get injured. But Sage and Noah were trained for this. I had to trust them.

I refocused on Noah to see how he was doing against the demon. The two of them were fighting faster than my eyes could follow. Noah was quick, but so was the demon. Each time I thought Noah was about to strike, the demon warded him off.

Whoever this demon was, he was a much better fighter than the ones we'd encountered in New Orleans and Charleston. He was quick and deadly—like he'd trained for this.

Noah finally got a strike in that pushed the knife out of the demon's hand and sent it colliding with the ground. He raised his slicer, about to straight through the demon's heart. But the demon moved away at the last second. With the element of surprise now on his side, the demon grabbed Noah's arm and threw him to the ground, prying the slicer from his hand and throwing it over his shoulder.

The slicer slammed into the wall beside me and fell to the ground.

If I'd been standing a few feet to the side, I'd be dead.

Noah's hands shifted into claws, his bones reshaping. He was shifting into wolf form. He wouldn't be able to kill the demon in wolf form—he'd need the slicer for that. But since he was stronger in wolf form, he'd at least be able to overpower the demon so he could *reach* the slicer and take another stab at him.

Before Noah completed his shift, the demon reached for his belt, brought out a potion pod, and threw it at him. It erupted into a sludge of brown.

I'd learned about a lot of the different potions during our long drives across the country. But I'd never heard of a potion that was *brown*.

When the haze from the potion pod dissipated, Noah was back in human form. The demon had gotten ahold of his knife again, and he had Noah pinned to the ground. His knife was inches above Noah's throat and getting lower by the second.

The brown potion must have stopped Noah from shifting.

I glanced at Sage. In situations like this, she was supposed to jump to the rescue. But she was covered in blood as she wrestled with the red-eyed wolf, looking no closer to beating it than before.

Suddenly, I heard an echo of Noah's voice inside my head. *Leave*, he said. He wasn't speaking, but I could hear him—no, it was more like I could *feel* him. He wanted me to hightail it out of there and go back to the hotel. He wanted me to know that he had this, and that it was too dangerous for me to stay.

I wasn't sure how I knew that. I just did.

I could also feel something else—something that I knew was coming from him and not from me.

Doubt.

He wasn't sure he could beat this demon. He was trying, but this demon was stronger than he was. It was almost like the demon had been prepared for an ambush.

There was a chance Noah wouldn't win this fight.

Terror rushed through my body. Noah might have wanted me to save myself, but I pushed back. I wasn't going to leave him and Sage here. They'd done so much for me. I'd be dead if it weren't for them, or kidnapped by demons. Sage was my friend. And Noah—well, I wasn't sure what was between us—but there was something. He might have denied it, but that kiss changed everything between us. As impossible as it sounded, it was almost like when we'd kissed, our souls had bound themselves to one another.

I couldn't stand there helplessly and watch them fight for their lives against these creatures. I had to do something.

But what? The wolf had teeth and claws that could shred me apart in seconds. And if I tried to use my boot knife against the demon, it wouldn't do anything since an angel hadn't blessed it with heavenly water. Yes, that stunt had worked with the coyotes. But this wasn't a coyote we were dealing with. It was a *demon*.

I glanced back over at the slicer laying a few feet away from me. My boot knife wouldn't hurt the demon —but the slicer would. And with the demon pinning Noah to the ground, I had *the* perfect chance to come at him from behind and ram the slicer through the demon's heart without him realizing what hit him.

The plan would be perfect—if the slicer didn't burn me when I touched it. Slicers were meant to be used by supernaturals—not by humans. They were too powerful for humans to handle. At least, that was Noah's guess about why the slicer had burned me. To warn me—a human—to *stay away*.

But I refused to stay away. Not when their lives were on the line like this. I didn't care that humans weren't supposed to use slicers. If anything happened to Noah or Sage—if either of them didn't make it tonight—I'd never be able to forgive myself for not trying to do the one thing that might have saved them.

So I reached down to grab the slicer, bracing myself for the inevitable burn the moment it touched my skin.

RAVEN

*F*ire.

A blaze of heat consumed me when I gripped the handle of the slicer. I was blinded by fire— by the pain. I saw red everywhere. My nerves burned— starting from my hands, and traveling through my entire body. It was like holding onto a hot coal, except the heat was somehow *inside me.*

I don't know how I managed not to scream.

I think it was because the element of surprise was all I had. If I screamed, the demon would know I was up to something. This would all be for nothing.

I had to fight through it. So I took one step forward, and then another. The heat was overwhelming—suffocating. Like hot tar covering my body. Boiling me alive. Beads of sweat gathered on my forehead and dripped to the ground next to my feet. The skin on my hands and arms started to bubble and blister.

I was burning alive from the inside out. The slicer was *killing* me.

I needed to drop it.

If I dropped it, the pain would stop.

Then I heard a grunt from where Noah and the demon were struggling. The demon still had Noah pinned to the ground. He lowered his knife further, the sharp edge of it against Noah's neck. Droplets of blood formed around it.

Noah's blood.

Shifters were strong, and they had the power to heal themselves. But they weren't invincible. Noah was pushing back at the demon to stop him from lowering the knife further. They were locked in a standstill. But if the demon sliced the knife through Noah's neck, Noah would die.

I refused to let that happen. The slicer was burning me alive, but I wouldn't let it win.

Hadn't Noah and Sage said that if I had any sort of "ability," it was pure stubbornness?

I needed to push through. Quickly—before I collapsed from the pain, and before the demon lowered that knife through Noah's neck.

So I ran. I ran toward the demon, even though it felt

like my raw, blistering skin was peeling away with every movement. Like my body was going to crack apart and break into pieces.

I got closer, and closer, until I was standing right behind the demon.

Noah's eyes widened when he saw me.

The demon's back was toward me, and he was so involved in his power struggle with Noah that he was oblivious to my presence.

The pain was so intense that spots clouded my vision, but I forced myself to focus. I had one chance to run the slicer through the demon's heart. I couldn't mess up.

The magic of the slicer—the same magic that was burning me alive—let it cut through muscle and bone like butter. So I didn't have to worry about the demon's ribcage or spine getting in the way. I just needed to aim in the right spot. If I missed the demon's heart, or if I didn't slam the slicer down hard enough, that was it. I'd lose my element of surprise and there would be no second chances.

But I knew how to use a knife. Noah had taught me during our training. And while I might not be strong, I had my body weight to work with.

Hopefully that would be enough. I just needed to

bear through the fiery pain for long enough to see it through.

I could do it. I'd gotten this far—I wasn't giving up now.

So I raised the knife in the air, putting the entire force of my weight behind it as I slammed it slightly left of the demon's spine. It cut through his flesh easily. I buried the blade in deep, as far as it could go, until only the hilt remained.

The demon turned to ash in a second. Since he'd been pinning Noah to the ground, I saw Noah through the dust of the demon's remains.

Noah's warm, brown eyes were the last things I saw before I dropped the slicer, toppling over and blacking out completely.

"*R*aven!" I screamed her name and reached for her, catching her in my arms before she hit the concrete.

Fear ripped through my heart as I looked down at her. Her skin was red and blistered, like she'd just walked through the fires of Hell. And no matter how many times I said her name, she was unresponsive.

I would have thought she was dead if I couldn't hear her beating heart. It was weak, but it was there. Thank God.

I needed to heal her.

Luckily, I was prepared for this. Raven acted tough, but as a human, she was more fragile than she knew.

Since she'd joined the hunt, I'd secretly been carrying around healing potion in case she needed it. My weapons belt didn't leave much space for potions—it could hold the teleporting potion I'd used against Azazel, plus one other.

With Raven tagging along, using the other spot for healing potion had been a no brainer.

I didn't want to set Raven down. But to give her the potion, I had to. So as gently as possible, I laid her down on the ground beside me. She didn't move or make a sound—she was out completely.

It was probably for the best. Being unconscious stopped her from feeling any pain. And judging from the severity of her burns, she would have been in a *lot* of pain.

I opened the pocket of my weapon belt and brought out the plastic vial full of light yellow liquid. But I cursed myself as I looked down at it.

Raven wouldn't be able to drink the potion, since she was unconscious.

I couldn't even get mad at myself for not bringing a potion pod, because a pod wouldn't have been enough to heal her injuries. Pods were the easiest way to deliver potions, but they weren't as strong. Drinking potions was ideal, since potions worked best from inside the body. Which was why I'd been carrying around the vial of healing potion.

But there was one other way to deliver potions. The

method commonly used on strong, unwilling super-naturals.

Injecting.

I didn't have any needles with me. But I *did* have two tranquilizer darts full of the anti-teleportation potion for greater demons.

I could work with that.

I pulled out one of the darts and pushed down on the syringe, squirting the light purple potion onto the ground. Once the dart was empty, I uncapped the vial, dipped the needle inside, and pulled on the syringe to fill it up. I worked slowly and methodically, trying to get as much of the yellow potion into the dart as possible.

As I worked, I couldn't get over the shock at what Raven had done. She'd wielded the slicer herself. The first time she'd tried to hold the slicer—back at the pool house—she hadn't been able to *touch* it because of the heat coming off of it.

Her current condition showed why.

She hadn't been able to touch the slicer because the magic in heavenly weapons was too powerful for humans to handle.

She should have bolted out of the alley and left me to battle the demon myself.

Why hadn't she run when I'd wanted her to? I used the imprint bond.

I supposed I was right that while I'd imprinted on Raven, she hadn't imprinted back. It explained why I'd been able to sense her desires through the imprint bond, but she hadn't been able to sense mine.

A wave of guilt overwhelmed me. I was responsible for Raven. I was the one who was supposed to keep her safe.

Yet, she'd risked her life for me.

She shouldn't have had to do that. That demon was stronger than any other I'd ever encountered—besides Azazel, of course—but that was no excuse. I was a trained fighter. I should have been able to overpower him.

I *would* have been able to overpower him... if he hadn't thrown that potion pod at me that had prevented me from shifting.

I'd heard of a spell that prevented shifters from shifting—like the one the rougarou had on the handcuffs when they'd captured us in New Orleans. It was a rare, dark magic spell. Only a witch as strong as the ones in the vampire kingdoms could cast it. All shifters had heard legends of such a spell, but those handcuffs were the first time I'd come across one.

A potion that stopped shifters from shifting was unheard of. It shouldn't exist.

Suddenly, someone appeared in front of me, nearly

interrupting my concentration as I finished filling up the needle.

Sage.

My need to help Raven had been so all consuming that I'd tuned out Sage fighting that strange shifter on the other side of the alley.

The shifter with the demonic red eyes.

I glanced at where they'd been fighting. The shifter was dead. I wasn't surprised—Sage was a tough fighter. Her brother had been training her to protect herself since before she could walk.

But despite the shifter's red eyes, it hadn't disappeared like the demons. That was an annoyance, but not the end of the world. We'd just have to make a call to the local witches so they could send a crew to deal with the body.

We'd do that after Raven was better, of course. I wouldn't be able to focus on *anything* until Raven was better.

"Noah?" Sage said my name as she kneeled down beside me, looking at Raven's burned skin in horror. "What happened?"

"I'll fill you in later," I said. "After she's healed."

I pricked the dart full of healing potion into Raven's arm and pushed down on the syringe, releasing the potion into her body. This wasn't an exact science—I didn't have to get it into a vein or anything. All that mattered was that the potion got inside of her body. From there, the magic would do its work and return Raven to the fiery, stubborn girl I knew and loved.

Once the dart was empty, I tossed it to the side and pulled Raven back into my arms.

I caressed her face, waiting for the red to fade from her skin—for the burns to return to normal.

"Come on." I rubbed the spot where I'd pricked her arm with the dart, as if that would help the potion circulate faster. "Get better." I repeated my desire for her to get better over and over again in my head, hoping to connect to the imprint bond and *will* her to heal. The connection I shared with her might not have worked when I'd wanted her to run from the alley, but I *needed* it to work this time.

Nothing happened.

My chest felt hollow, and it hurt to breathe.

It should have started working by now.

"We need more healing potion," I said. "It must not have been enough."

"Noah." Sage placed her hand gently on my arm. "I'm so sorry. You know healing potion doesn't work if—"

"Stop." I glared at her, cutting her off before she could continue. Because I had a pretty good feeling about what she was going to say.

Healing potion doesn't work if the wounds are fatal.

But I could still hear Raven's heartbeat. It was weaker than usual, but it was there. Yes, her skin was badly burned, but the healing potion should have been able to heal a surface level injury like that.

Unless... no one knew what happened when a human held a heavenly weapon for so long, let alone used it to kill a demon. What if her skin wasn't all that was burned?

What if her insides were burned, too?

It would explain why the healing potion wasn't working.

Just thinking about the possibility made me feel like I was crumbling to pieces.

This couldn't be the end. I knew I hadn't wanted to tell Raven about the imprint—I'd given Sage a lot of excuses about why that was, but none of those reasons were true.

The truth was that I hadn't wanted to tell Raven about the imprint because I feared she hadn't imprinted back. My life so far had been a series of disappointments. Women tended to see me as a guy who was good for a bit of fun in the moment, but not for long term. They always had someone else out there—a soul mate who was the perfect match for them to spend their lives with.

Someone who *wasn't* me.

I didn't think I could handle another disappointment like that. Especially not from someone who ignited my emotions as much as Raven.

The truth was that I was falling in love with Raven, and it absolutely terrified me.

Now, holding her dying body, I regretted my decision not to tell her about the imprint more than ever. Because while I knew it was unlikely… what if she *had* imprinted back?

I'd only know if I was honest with her. So I swore to the angels up in Heaven—if Raven survived this, I'd tell her everything. If she didn't return my feelings, so be it. At least I'd know I tried.

With that decision, I shifted back into focus. Because sitting here sulking wasn't going to save Raven's life. If she was going to live, I needed to get with the program and take action to make that happen.

"Run and get the car from the hotel," I told Sage, quickly switching gears into focus mode. "Drive it back here and pick us up. I'll carry Raven out of this alley and wait for you on the street."

With Sage's supernatural speed, I imagined it should take her a few minutes, tops. I'd nearly told her to find the closest car on the street and hotwire it, but if the police got on our tails, it would waste precious time we didn't have.

"Why?" she asked. "Where are we going?"

"We're going back to the local witches in Brentwood," I said. "And they're going to save Raven—even if they have to use the darkest magic in their arsenal to do it."

RAVEN

I was back in the cell—the same cell from the nightmare I'd had the first night I'd stayed with Noah in the pool house. The walls were made of rock, and the floor was dirt.

The cell was part of a cave. A cave transformed into some kind of underground prison.

At least, it seemed like I was underground, from the lack of windows and the condensation on the rock walls.

I wasn't alone. Well, I was alone in the cell, but there were other cells nearby, and two of them were occupied. I recognized the occupants from my previous dream. The chubby, homely woman in the cell next to me stared down at her tray of food. Only bars separated our cells, as if whoever built this place was too lazy to build actual walls. She absently stirred her bowl of oatmeal, staring at the glass of water beside it. Her eyes were empty—as if all the life had been sucked from her soul.

The beautiful woman in the sparkly clubbing outfit still occupied the cell across from mine. Her dress was covered with so much dirt and grime that it had lost its sparkle. She sat hunched down on the floor, leaning against the wall with her hands splayed out beside her. Her lips were stained red, a few drops of it on her chin.

Next to her was the bloodied body of a dead squirrel.

Had she been eating the squirrel?

"What are you staring at?" She sneered. "Does my lunch look better to you than yours?"

I glanced at my lunch—it was on a tray to my side. Oatmeal and a glass of water. Well, I guessed the bowl had once been full of oatmeal, since that was what was the lady next to me had. My bowl was licked clean.

Before leaving for Europe, oatmeal had been one of my go-to breakfasts. It was easy to make and healthy.

Since getting back home, I hadn't touched it. Just the sight of it made my stomach swirl.

Suddenly, the pieces started to fit into place. Because when I was gone, I hadn't been in Europe. The rougarou had told me that my memories had been erased and replaced. They didn't know where I'd been. But the memories had to be somewhere in my mind, buried beneath the surface and trying to claw their way out.

The last time I'd had this dream, I'd thought it was just that—a dream.

Now that I was back here, and now that I knew my trip to Europe had never happened, I was starting to see this vision for what it truly was.

A memory.

All of this was real. It had actually happened.

Could I control what I did here? Or was I just an onlooker to my memories, unable to participate in them?

There was only one way to find out.

"Why are we here?" I asked the girl across from me—the one who had been eating the raw squirrel. "Who locked us up here?"

Good. I could interact with the dream... or vision... or memory. Whatever it was, I could control my actions while here.

"Seriously?" The girl rolled her eyes. "Did Geneva slip some memory potion into your oatmeal today?"

"Geneva..." I repeated the name. It sounded so familiar.

A picture of what Geneva looked like was on the edge of my mind. I tried to reach for it, but it remained fuzzy.

Why couldn't I remember who she was?

"Stop getting distracted, Raven." The woman from the cell next to me spoke up. Her voice was harsh and creepy, and she stared at me with wide, alert eyes, like she was a ghost in a horror movie. "Your subconscious brought you here—to this

exact moment—for a reason. Watch. Listen. Learn. Your life depends on it."

The alertness vanished from her eyes, and she turned away from me to continue staring blankly at her glass of water.

Then she reached for it, dumped the water onto the ground, and threw the glass against the rock wall behind her.

It shattered, the shards falling to the ground.

"Susan!" I screamed her name. The words came out of my mouth so easily that I realized it was something I'd actually said when this was all happening—not something I was controlling now. "What are you doing? You can't waste your water like that. You need it."

"I'm done." She walked over to the pieces of glass and picked one up—a shard so sharp that it glimmered in the little light that we had down here. "I doubt we'll ever be let out of here. Even if we are, I don't want to go back. Not now that I know what monsters are out there. So I'm getting myself out of this hellhole. Judge me all you want, but it won't be long until you'll want to do the same."

"What are you talking about?" Horror filled me down to my bones. "What are you going to do?"

She stared and me pityingly and smiled. "I'm getting myself out of here," she said. "I'll see you on the other side."

Before I could plead with her to stop, she brought the glass down to her wrist and dragged it across her skin. Blood poured *out of the wound faster than I thought possible. She must have been running on pure adrenaline, because she transferred the glass to her injured hand and repeated the same thing on her other wrist, digging in just as deep.*

She dropped the shard and slid down to the ground, balancing her arms on her knees as she stared at the blood seeping out of her wrists. The blood dripped down along her legs, collecting in a puddle on the ground.

I screamed and ran to the bars at the front of my cell. "Geneva!" I yelled, since I knew she was still in there. She always came to collect our dirty dishes—and to collect our blood—after we finished our daily meal. "We need help! Susan needs help! You need to come back! Now!"

The girl across from me also ran to the front of her cell and was gripping the bars. She pulled at them so hard it was a miracle they didn't rip right off.

But she wasn't screaming for help. No—she'd gone completely feral. Her eyes were wide with hunger, and she snarled at Susan, her fangs out as she stared at the growing puddle of blood at the woman's feet.

Her fangs. The girl across from me wasn't a human.

She was a vampire.

I knew vampires existed. Noah and Sage had told me about them early on in our hunt.

But this was the first vampire I'd ever seen. And her fangs, her chin with the squirrel blood still on it, and the way she was going feral at the sight of Susan's blood was unnerving, to say the least.

If it hadn't been for the bars keeping her in—the bars that must be extraordinarily strong, to resist her vampire strength —she would have run right over to Susan and finished her off. Judging by how hungry she looked, I'd probably be next.

Suddenly, someone appeared in the hallway between the cells. A petite woman who looked like she'd come straight from the 1920s in her flapper dress and her dark hair perfectly styled in a bob cut.

Geneva.

*N*ow that I saw her, I remembered Geneva from the last dream I'd had. Well, the last memory I'd had.

It was pretty clear by now that these visions were memories, not dreams.

Geneva took one look at Susan and shook her head. "Oh, Susan." She sounded like a mother who'd walked in on her kid making a mess in the house. "Did you really think you'd succeed in offing yourself before I found you?"

Susan simply stared at her, saying nothing.

"You didn't even cut deep enough to hit a major artery," Geneva continued. "At this rate, it's going to take you hours to bleed out."

"Make it quicker," Susan begged, letting her arms flop to her sides. "Please."

"I'm afraid I can't do that," Geneva said. *"Because I need you alive. So I'm going to keep you that way."*

"You're going to use one of those devil potions to save me, aren't you?" Susan sounded devoid of life, as if being saved were the worst fate she could imagine.

"Of course not." Geneva shook her head in disappointment. *"There's no point in wasting perfectly good healing potion on fatal wounds. Especially when there's another, much simpler option."* She whisked something small out of her pocket—a dart gun—turned around, and aimed it at the vampire in the cell across from me.

Stephenie. That was the name of the vampire in the cell. Princess Stephenie. Of the vampire kingdom of the Vale.

The dart hit Stephenie straight in the neck. She sucked in a deep, painful breath, and collapsed to the floor.

"Wormwood." Geneva smiled and looked down at the vampire's body. *"Gets them every time."*

I gripped the bars in shock. *"Did you kill her?"* I asked.

"No," Geneva said. *"I need her for the same reason I need the two of you."*

"And what reason is that?" I doubted she would answer, but there was no harm in trying.

"Do you really think I'm going to tell you?" She laughed. *"Anyway, she's not dead. I just knocked her out so I can take what I need from her."* She flashed out of existence for a few seconds and then reappeared inside of Stephenie's cell holding

a tube to draw blood. She leaned down, poked the needle into Stephenie's elbow, and filled up the tube.

Once full, she tucked it away in her pocket, then removed another empty tube and filled that one up as well. With the tube full of blood in hand, she teleported into Susan's cell and stood over the dying woman.

She reached down to touch Susan's shoulder and teleported both of them into the cell next to Stephenie's. "I'll keep you here until your cell is cleaned up," she said. "No more glass for you. Your meals will be thoroughly child proofed from now on. Now, open up."

She leaned down and pried Susan's mouth open with one hand. With the other hand, she uncapped the vial of Stephenie's blood and dumped it down Susan's throat. Then she held Susan's mouth closed, forcing the older woman to swallow.

Once she was done, she took a step back. "Don't force yourself to throw it up," she said. "If you do, I'll just get more and inject it."

She teleported back into the hallway, her eyes locked on Susan.

I watched Susan as well, my mouth dropping open as the wounds on her arms started to close. They were healed in a minute—as if they'd never been there in the first place.

Susan stood up and looked around in a daze, touching her arms to examine her healed skin. "You," she growled at Geneva. "What did you do to me?" She ran at the bars with supernatural speed, gripping them and yanking them with as much force as Stephenie had earlier. "Did you turn me into one of those... things?" She glanced at Stephenie when she said the final word—the vampire princess was still motionless on the floor.

That wormwood stuff had knocked her out cold.

"Of course not," Geneva said. "You'd make a terrible vampire. Not that it would matter, since I doubt you'd survive the change. But it's a little known fact that when a human drinks vampire blood, any injuries they have will heal. Even if the injury's fatal. There will be some side effects—you'll have the abilities of a vampire for twenty-four hours, and a nasty hangover when the high of the vampire blood wears off. But you'll be alive."

"Wow." I leaned forward, my hands still wrapped around my cell bars. "That's amazing. Think of all the people that could save..."

I thought about all the humans in hospitals dying from fatal injuries. A bit of vampire blood, and they'd be cured.

It was incredible.

"Which is exactly why vampires keep the healing properties of their blood a secret," Geneva said. "They can't risk being hunted and harvested for their blood. Not even other supernaturals know what their blood can do."

"Then how do you know?" I asked.

"I have my ways," she said mysteriously.

"And you don't mind that Susan and I know?" Since the power of vampire blood was such a well-kept secret, I figured she needed Susan and I alive pretty desperately to risk giving the secret away to us.

"At the end of all of this, you and Susan will either be dead or given memory potion to forget this ever happened," she said. "I haven't decided yet. But if you cooperate—meaning no more antics like trying to kill yourselves—I'll be more likely to go with the second option. So from now on, I recommend you stay on your best behavior. Understood?"

Then she disappeared from the room, and as she did, I faded out of the memory as well.

RAVEN

*P*ain.

That was all I felt when I came to. Searing, blinding pain that consumed me from my skin down to my bones.

Except I couldn't move or speak. I couldn't even scream. It was like I was trapped in my own body, halfway between the real world and the memory I'd just left.

I was laid out on what felt like a table, and I heard voices around me.

"I'm sorry," a woman said.

Was she the witch from the Nashville circle we'd gone to earlier that day? It sounded like it.

"There was, of course, a chance you didn't give her enough healing potion earlier," she continued. "But you watched me give her another full dose right here. It didn't work. Her wounds are fatal. There's unfortunately nothing more I can do."

She was talking about me. I didn't know how I knew —I just did.

Maybe because I was laid out on a table in so much pain that it felt like I was dying.

"No." Noah was near—right next to me—and he was angry. "There has to be something else you can do. Anything. Even if it's dark magic… you have to save her. Please."

"I'm sorry," the witch said again. "There's nothing that can be done—not even with dark magic. Trust me, if there were I'd be happy to sell it to you."

"So what do we do?" Sage asked.

"I recommend saying your goodbyes," the witch replied. "Look at her—she must be in so much pain. It's a miracle she stayed alive this long. It'll be a blessing for her once she passes over. She won't be in pain anymore."

Passes over? Did she mean *die*?

I was so *not* going to die. Not yet. I had so much left to do. I had to get to Avalon, I had to get through the Angel Trials, and I had to save my mom.

Yes, I was in pain. But I refused to give into it. I was going to fight. I was going to *live*.

But how?

That was when I remembered—the dream. No—the *memory*.

Vampire blood could heal me.

I must have flashed back to that specific moment so I'd remember the secret about vampire blood. My body must have known I was dying and somehow forced the memory to come back.

I also remembered something else—only vampires knew what their blood could do. They kept it secret from all other supernaturals.

I needed to tell Noah, Sage, and the witch. They couldn't use vampire blood to heal me if they didn't know it was possible.

Except I couldn't *move*, let alone speak.

I tried to fight it—tried to fight through the pain. But no matter what I did, I was stuck. Trapped. It was like when I'd touched that heavenly knife, I'd fried all my nerves so I could no longer move. It was like my body wasn't mine anymore.

"No," Noah said, and I felt something wet splash onto my arm. A tear? "She can't die. I can't lose her."

"Did you love her?" the witch asked.

I hated how she was speaking about me in past tense. She needed to stop doing that. Because I was here. I wasn't dead yet.

Noah didn't reply. Which was a shame, since I was curious about his answer myself.

I'd never know his answer if I didn't tell them about the vampire blood. I just needed control of my body for a few seconds. A few seconds, and I could tell them how to cure me.

But maybe I didn't need to *speak* to tell him.

Maybe I could manifest it.

It was crazy, yes. But it worked when the rougarou had captured us. And when Noah was fighting the demon, I had a feeling he was manifesting his desire for me to run away onto me. Because there was no way that thought had been my own.

There was some kind of connection between our minds—it had been there since he'd kissed me in New Orleans.

And I was going to use it to save my life.

Vampire blood, I thought, willing him to receive my message with every inch of my being. *If you give me vampire blood, it'll heal me.*

I thought it over and over, imagining the words floating through the air and entering Noah's mind. It felt like it was taking forever, but I continued repeating the thought anyway.

I wouldn't give up until I was dead.

"Vampire blood," I finally heard Noah say. "If we give her vampire blood, it'll heal her."

I wished I could jump up and hug him. No—I wished I could jump up and *kiss* him.

Instead, I faded into unconsciousness again, glad to be free of the pain—and relieved that Noah and Sage now had the knowledge they needed to save my life.

"What are you talking about?" Sage asked. "How can vampire blood heal her?"

"Raven communicated with me through the imprint bond," I said. "She said that vampire blood could heal her."

"Imprint bond?" Gayle—the Nashville witch who was working with us—gasped. "But you're a shifter. She's a human..." She looked between me and Raven, wariness in her eyes. "How's that possible?"

"It's a long story," I said, since I didn't have time to explain it—and since I didn't have any answers myself. "Have you ever heard about vampire blood being able to heal humans? Even from fatal injuries?"

"Never," she said.

"Well, it's worth a shot." I spoke quickly, since we had no time to waste. "If it works, we'll save Raven's life. And if it doesn't, then at least we tried. So where can we find vampires in this town?"

Sage took a deep breath and watched me closely, her eyes sad. "We can't just go up to a random vampire and ask for their blood," she said.

"Why not?" I glared at her. I'd do anything to save Raven, and I thought Sage was on my side.

"Because no one's ever heard of vampire blood being able to heal humans," she said. "If it's true—which for Raven's sake, I hope it is—then the vampires are keeping the healing property of their blood a secret. They've been keeping it a secret for *centuries*. If we go to a vampire we can't trust and reveal that know we know this secret, they'll kill us."

I frowned, since Sage had a point. I mean, I could hold my own against a single vampire, but...

With that thought, an idea crossed my mind. But I couldn't say it in front of Gayle.

"Would you mind leaving us alone for a few minutes?" I asked the witch.

"No problem," she said. "As long as you don't touch anything. If anything in here is broken or gone when I return, you'll be billed double its worth."

"Understood," I said.

The witch gave Raven one last pitying look, then left us alone in the apothecary.

"You have a plan," Sage said. "And I'm not going to like it."

She knew me too well.

"We'll find a vampire that's alone," I said, blocking out all feelings about what I was going to say next. "We'll take their blood for Raven, and then we'll silence them."

"Silence them?" She looked at me like she didn't know me. "You mean *kill them?*"

"It's our only option." I squeezed Raven's hand—I hadn't let go of it the entire time we'd been here. "I can't lose her. I just... can't."

"You're wrong." Sage crossed her arms and looked at me in challenge. "Because there *is* another option. We can go to a vampire we trust."

"There are no vampires I trust." My most recent experience with a vampire—Princess Karina of the Carpathian Kingdom—had solidified my less than stellar opinion of the species. "Except for Prince Jacen, but he's in Avalon and we can't get to Avalon yet. Not without killing one more demon first. And by the time we find a demon, hunt it down, kill it, and get to the Vale... well, I don't think Raven will make it that long.

Besides, I'm not leaving her alone in this condition. So this is it. We'll do it my way. You don't have to come with me. Just promise me you'll watch over Raven, and let me handle it. All right?"

"No can do," she said. "Because while there might not be any vampires *you* trust, there does happens to be a vampire *I* trust."

"Oh yeah?" I'd never heard Sage say anything positive about vampires. She'd always shared my opinion that they were conniving, manipulative, cold-hearted creatures. So the fact that she trusted even *one* of them was a shock, to say the least.

"The Bettencourt vampires." Her eyes went hard as she mentioned them—as if speaking about them pained her. "More specifically, the leader of their coven. Thomas Bettencourt."

There was a long, painful story behind her relationship with this man—Thomas Bettencourt. I could see it in her eyes.

But I couldn't waste time asking questions. If Sage said she trusted this man, I believed her.

"We don't know how much longer Raven has," I said. "Where's the Bettencourt coven located?"

If they weren't close enough, I'd revert to my previous plan to find a nearby vampire and kill him for his blood myself. I wouldn't feel good about it—no one deserved to die for no reason, including vampires—but I'd feel worse if I lost Raven.

Maybe that made me selfish. But right now, I didn't care.

All I cared about was saving her.

"They're in Chicago," she said. "Which is approximately…" She brought her phone out and did a search. "Seven hours from here."

"Seven hours." I touched Raven's charred face, hating that it had come to this. It tore me up to see her in so much pain. She'd done this to herself for me, and now there was a chance I could lose her.

She deserved so much more. She deserved to *live*.

"Do you think you can hold on for seven hours?" I wasn't sure if she could hear me, but it was worth a try.

Her heartbeat strengthened slightly, and I felt a surge of brightness through the imprint bond. Hope and determination.

Raven wanted us to bring her to the Bettencourt vampires.

"Noah?" Sage said softly. "What are you thinking?"

"I'm thinking we have no time to waste." I picked Raven up off the table and pulled her to my chest, trying to send as much strength to her through the imprint bond as possible.

She would make it. She *had* to make it.

Then I looked at Sage, confident that now, we had a real chance to save Raven's life. "Come on," I said, cradling Raven's limp body to my chest as I walked toward the door. "We're going to Chicago."

THOMAS

I was lounging in my penthouse apartment that looked over the Chicago skyline, drinking my evening cup of blood while watching the human news, when my phone rang with a call from Flint Montgomery.

I hadn't heard from the Montgomery alpha in years.

Curiosity got the best of me. The human news had been fascinating recently—violence had increased in the past few months, which I assumed was an effect of the demons that had been unleashed onto the Earth. Every day it seemed like there was another robbery, shooting, or hate crime. The demons were bringing out the worst in humanity, and it wasn't pretty.

It was also only going to get worse from here.

But despite my interest in the news, a call from Flint

was far more fascinating. So I turned off the television and accepted his call.

"Flint Montgomery." I always liked to be the first to speak. It asserted my dominance, even over the alpha of a powerful shifter pack. "To what do I owe this pleasure?"

"I need your help." Flint sounded different—more *erratic* than usual. "It's about Sage."

"Oh?" I took a sip of blood, trying to cool the rush of emotions that flooded my mind whenever I thought about Sage Montgomery. "What type of trouble has my favorite shifter gotten herself into now?"

"She's run off," Flint said. "With the First Prophet of the Vale."

"He's alive?" Disgust wracked my body at the mention of the infamous First Prophet. "I thought he was killed in the battle at the Vale."

"He survived," Flint confirmed. "And he's brainwashed Sage into running off with him."

By now, every vampire knew the story about how months ago, an ancient demon soul had possessed a witch's body and allied with the wolves of the Vale. The First Prophet was the first of the wolves of the Vale to receive dreams from the demon—he believed the demon was some sort of *savior* for the wolves.

So he'd welcomed the possessed witch into his pack.

With the witch's help, he'd gathered the numerous packs in the Vale to war against the vampires they shared their land with. Once the ground was soaked with supernatural blood, the witch was able to do the spell to open the Hell Gate, releasing hundreds of demons onto the Earth.

The First Prophet had played a huge part in getting us into this mess with the demons in the first place.

How had Sage managed to get involved with *him*?

I downed the rest of my blood quickly, needing the strength for the rest of this conversation.

"Don't tell me," I said, fearing the worst. "She's imprinted on him."

"No." Flint sounded just as disgusted by the possibility as I felt. "Nothing like that."

I was relieved—but only slightly. "Then why's she with him?" I asked.

"He's convinced her to join him on this insane hunt around the country to kill demons," he said. "He says that once he kills enough of them, he'll be allowed entrance to Avalon."

"And you think he's lying?" I asked.

"I *know* he's lying," Flint said. "The Earth Angel would never let the First Prophet into Avalon. The quest to kill demons was never his, and neither is the heavenly weapon he's using to kill them with. The quest belonged to one of the coyotes of the Southwest Texas pack. Noah

—that's the First Prophet's given name—was so desperate to get to Avalon that he killed the coyote shifter, stole his heavenly weapon, and made the quest his own. He's stuck under some insane delusion that if he can complete the quest, the Earth Angel will change her mind about him and accept him onto the island."

"That does sound rather insane," I agreed.

"The First Prophet assisted in opening the Hell Gate," Flint said. "He's not in his right mind. And now he has my sister convinced that he's some kind of anti-hero on a quest for salvation."

"Sage always had a weakness for anti-heroes in need of salvation," I said bitterly.

"Then you understand how she could get mixed up in all of this," Flint said. "But I need Sage home, with me. I'm not supposed to tell anyone this—so you need to keep it between us—but the Montgomery pack is in the middle of making an alliance that will keep us safe in the upcoming war. The alliance will be made official in a week. If Sage isn't home by then, she'll be left out of the alliance forever."

Flint normally wasn't a man of this many words. So I listened, but the more he continued, the more I wondered what he wasn't telling me.

"Sage knows about this alliance, yet she's staying on the run with the First Prophet?" I asked.

"She isn't of her right mind," Flint said. "The First Prophet is a talented manipulator. She's convinced that she needs to help him. But what do you think will happen once he goes to Avalon and tries to get credit for completing a quest that wasn't his? I can't say for myself, but I doubt the Earth Angel will take kindly to what he's done—nor will she look kindly on his co-conspirators. Which is why I need Sage out of this mess and home where she belongs."

"I understand," I said, worry coursing through my veins at the thought of Sage out there with the First Prophet of the Vale. "But what, exactly, do I have to do with this?"

"I have it on good authority that Sage, the First Prophet, and a human pet they've been keeping with them will be heading to Chicago soon," he said. "Specifically, they'll be heading straight to your doorstep."

I didn't bother asking how he knew this. The Montgomery alpha wouldn't reveal his sources to me, just like I wouldn't reveal any of mine to him. "You want me to try talking some sense into her?" I asked. "Convince her to part ways with the First Prophet?"

"That won't be enough," he said. "If you *truly* want Sage to be safe, then you'll kill the First Prophet and his human pet, and bring Sage to me."

He sounded eager—overly so.

I'd learned from experience that it was best to be on guard whenever someone sounded too eager. Especially when they wanted someone dead.

"I'm glad you called," I said, since it was best I remained neutral until I had more information. "You know I want Sage safe just as much as you do."

"So we're in agreement, then."

"We are," I said. "I'll call you once I've made progress, but Sage will be safe in my hands, and her companions will be appropriately taken care of. I don't make promises lightly, but I can promise you that."

Once we ended the call, I stared out at the glittering skyline, contemplating how to proceed. I was looking forward to seeing Sage—each year I hadn't seen her had torn at my heart in ways I hadn't expected. Despite the way I'd ended things with her, I'd never stopped thinking about her. I didn't think I ever would.

But I had to push my feelings for Sage to the side for now.

Because Flint was hiding something. Something big. Something that involved Sage.

And whatever he was hiding, I was going to get to the bottom of it.

Thank you for reading The Angel Hunt! I hope you loved this book as much as I loved writing it. The next book in the series—The Angel Trap—will release in Summer 2018. It'll be jam packed with even more romance, adventure, and twists. I can't wait for you to read it!

To receive an email alert from me when The Angel Trap releases, visit www.michellemadow.com/subscribe and sign up for my newsletter.

If you haven't read the first season of the Dark World Saga yet—The Vampire Wish—I recommend checking it out while you're waiting for the next installment in the Angel Trials series. If you're curious about what happened to Noah when he was the First Prophet of the Vale, the answers are in The Vampire Wish series. And the best part is—the series starts with a FREEBIE, The Vampire Rules!

Go to www.michellemadow.com/freevampirerules to grab The Vampire Rules and start reading it now. To get the freebie, you'll be subscribing to my newsletter. I love connecting with my readers and promise not to spam you. But you're free to unsubscribe at any time <3

ABOUT THE AUTHOR

Michelle Madow is a USA Today bestselling author of fast paced fantasy novels that will leave you turning the pages wanting more! Her books are full of magic, adventure, romance, and twists you'll never see coming.

To get free books, exclusive content, and instant updates from Michelle, visit www.michellemadow.com/subscribe and subscribe to her newsletter now!

THE ANGEL HUNT

Published by Dreamscape Publishing

ISBN: 1718904606
ISBN-13: 978-1718904606

❀ Created with Vellum

Made in the USA
Middletown, DE
15 February 2019